*In memory of my mother
who wrote every day of her life*

Published in the United States of America

Mystery/Crime/Fiction
Women's Fiction/Crime
9.22.15

Paperback ISBN: 978-9908351-3-4
eBook ISBN: 978-0-9908351-1-0

THE CABIN BY THE SEA

THE AUDREY MURDERS

LEONIE MATEER

CHAPTER 1

Gavin leaned across the table and grabbed the morning paper. He was not computer literate and preferred to find what he wanted in the classified section of the paper. He flicked through the pages until he found 'Properties for Rent.' Peering through his cheap reading glasses he started going down the list. Nothing. As usual there was nothing that appealed to him. He noticed his coffee had gone cold and headed off towards the coffee pot for a refill.

He heard his sister in the next room getting ready for work. Gavin knew he had outstayed his welcome and very soon she would ask him to leave. He dreaded moving out. He had nowhere to go and no one to go to. His future had disappeared into his past. Divorce, retirement and homelessness had unfortunately coincided, leaving Gavin at the mercy of his sister's benevolence.

"Gavin," he heard his sister calling, "Gavin, where are you?" He could hear the irritation in her voice. She appeared in the kitchen all pumped up and pompous. Her long, straight blonde hair flowed over her wide shoulders and down her broad back. His sister had eaten her way into a lonely existence. Her once slim physique had drawn men like bees to honey. Gavin thought she was probably a lesbian in denial. She had no children, no pets and in her later years had started hoarding. At first it was little things like newspapers and magazines kept in piles in the spare bedroom. He could tell she wanted him to leave so she didn't have to hide her frustration at having him in her precious space - spaces that needed to be filled.

"What is it?" he asked.

"I have been checking online and found the perfect place for you," she said with sheer glee. "It is quiet, fully furnished and overlooks the ocean. It sounds just what you have been looking for."

Gavin thought she had no idea what he was looking for. If he didn't know, how could she possibly know? His sister produced a sheet of paper with the property details along with a photo of a little cabin surrounded by lawns and trees. "I have already emailed them and arranged time for you to view it," she said.

Gavin took the paper and began to read.

A Cabin by the Sea
Private, secluded and fully furnished
14 acres of native bush * overlooking the ocean
Suitable for one adult
$200.00 per week
No pets, No smoking, No children
Owner lives on property in separate cottage

Gavin put the paper in his pocket and filled his empty cup

with hot brewed coffee. He may as well check it out. The price was right, and the seclusion was what he was looking for. And, better yet, he could get out of here where he wasn't welcome.

Chapter 2

T he driveway was lined in the tallest pine trees Audrey had ever seen. They were planted so close together that a few dead ones simply rested on stronger healthier trees. They leaned precariously inward towards the driveway creating a sinister threat to anyone daring to drive the long distance to the cottages.

It had taken her six months and every penny she had managed to recoup from the sale of her chalets to renovate the dilapidated cabins and release the view from the old gnarly pine trees which had grown like weeds on the hillside and now lay spread eagled on the bush floor.

A secondhand mower took care of the lawns around the two buildings and four sheep took care of the newly exposed acres of freshly sown grass and clover. Audrey still had to take care of the fencing situation as the pro kiwi Nazis had threatened to shoot them on a number of occasions when they had been spotted wandering aimlessly up the steep gravel road in the search of fresher grass and tastier morsels.

As she pulled up in front of the little white cottage with a bright red awning she took a moment to soak in the beautiful ocean view. Perched high on the hill she could see for miles. Karikari peninsular was in the distance and the red sandy beaches of Cable Bay contrasted with the deep blue shades of a quiet ocean. A lone fisherman was fishing off his kayak not far from the shore. Pleasure boats buzzed in the twinkling water. She reached over for her handbag forcing herself away from the quiet moment, knowing she had to face a new reality.

For weeks now she had made the trip from The Three Suites to her new home. Each time bringing boxes filled with unwanted and long forgotten keepsakes. Everything of value she had owned was now the property of the new owners. All her furniture, books, music, DVDs, pots, pans, rugs and linens were now just memories.

She forced open the weathered glass door and walked inside. The secondhand furniture was a sorry replacement for her previous life of luxury and wealth. She opened up several boxes on the kitchen floor and began to unpack worn linens rescued from The Three Suites so she could make her bed. Tomorrow would be a better day. Audrey had arranged to meet a man who was interested in renting the cabin. A man she was hoping would be just the perfect tenant. And, if so, he might just be her next project.

CHAPTER 3

Audrey peeked through the cream linen curtain at the car coming up the gravel driveway. She had heard him stop at the gate and hoped he had closed it behind him so the sheep would not escape again. Audrey had never met her neighbors and she didn't care to. She just knew she had pissed them off by her sheep constantly absconding. There were only a handful of residents on the peninsula and, like her, they were all neatly tucked away down long driveways with bolted wooden gates with private property deterrent signs.

Her bruised self-esteem had taken a severe beating since she had sold The Three Suites at a terrible loss. But she had managed to scrape through the past year with just enough money to renovate the two old cabins on Tiromoana; her family's fourteen acre neglected property. She hoped this was a suitable tenant for the cabin pulling up to her recently graveled parking area.

Audrey tucked a loose strand of bleached blonde hair under a hairpin and made her way up the path to greet her new guest.

"You must be Gavin. Welcome to Tiromoana. I hope you had a pleasant drive here." She looked with interest at the tall lean

6

man in his late fifties. He reached out his hand in anticipation of a formal welcome.

"Nice to meet you" he said as Audrey grabbed his hand in an enthusiastic squeeze. "Found it no trouble. Good directions. You have a great view here. Just what I am looking for." He said enthusiastically.

Audrey led the way to the cabin and through the open door and watched as the man's eyes wandered over the freshly painted interior with light timber beams and snap-together fake- wood panel flooring. The furniture was fresh and cosy and she had decorated the walls with original paintings of seaside landscapes. Audrey was proud of the results. Secondhand kitchen cupboards and furniture was all she could afford but she had managed to create respectable accommodation for any discerning tenant.

This was her fourth applicant for the cabin. She had quickly rejected the other three online. She didn't want anyone with a family or small children. The cabin was really only suitable for one adult and the right tenant had to be as reclusive as her. Since her financial ruin she hated to socialize. Making small talk and pretending life was wonderful only made her feel more alienated from the world. She just wished she didn't need to share her isolation with someone else. But it would not be forever. It had been far too long since her last "project."

Her thoughts were interrupted by the man's question. "Is there good fishing here?

"Yes, she said. We have a private road to the rocky beach which is great for fishing."

"Two hundred dollars per week you are asking?"

"Yes, paid monthly in advance with a one month's deposit. Why don't I leave you to look around? I will be in the cottage next door," Audrey suggested as she made her way across the short distance between the two buildings.

CHAPTER 4

Gavin sat at the small square wood table and looked around the one-roomed cabin. The queen bed sat at one end with a small blue painted side table. He thought the big blue lazy boy chair looked quite comfortable and admired the new LCD flat screen television perched atop an old chest of drawers. He opened the door to the small bathroom and was disappointed there were only a shower and not a bath. But the room looked clean and well organized. The kitchen was fully stocked. There was everything he would need, an oven, microwave, washing machine, kitchen pots and pans, crockery, cutlery. He pulled back the curtains and exposed a large wardrobe. He grimaced as he remembered how little he actually owned. A couple of pairs of jeans, a winter jacket, rain gear, some sweatshirts and a few pairs of boots were thrown in the back of his car along with a fishing rod, crayfish pot and an old tin box.

He walked outside to the wood-stained deck. A couple of wood benches and a green plastic table sat on the far end of the deck. Big potted plants sat either side of the sliding door. The view from the cabin was more rural. Freshly mowed lawns, fruit trees, tall pine trees and random fences marked the boundary around the two buildings. The ocean view was further across the property towards the front of the cottage. He wondered if he would be allowed to use the table and chairs overlooking the ocean or if they were out of bounds to the cabin tenant. He must ask the owner. He wandered over to the little white cottage and found her sitting outside.

"I'll take it," he said. "How soon can I move in?"

"As soon as you like," said Audrey.

"Is now, OK?" He asked presumptuously. "I have a four-hour drive back to my sister's house where I have been staying and I would much prefer just to settle in today."

"I am rather reclusive," Audrey said, eyeing him up and down. "I am looking for someone who also prefers to live in peace and quiet. Do you know the area up here?"

"Can't say I do" he replied. "I am just looking for a quiet place to live and do some fishing. I can pay you in cash for the deposit and the first month's rent. Would that be acceptable?"

Audrey knew she would not find a more suitable tenant. She said she would organize the lease agreement while he moved his belongings into the cabin. After all, Audrey needed the money and he obviously needed somewhere to live immediately. She made her way inside to find a blank rental agreement. Her bright green eyes watched curiously as the man made his way over to his parked car. He was not an unattractive man, but she could tell he was on hard times. His gaunt appearance and disheveled clothing could not hide his obvious good upbringing. He spoke with an educated voice and his manner seemed pleasant and respectful.

The man removed a couple of bags from his car and made his way into the cabin. He returned to remove a fishing line and tackle box and placed them on the wood deck.

Audrey walked over to meet him. "There is a shop about ten

minutes north from here" she said. "I guess you will need to pick up some supplies."

"Great" he said. "I will head out there shortly. First, I would like to wander down to the beach and check out the fishing spots." Audrey gave him directions to their private road to the waterfront and handed him the rental agreement.

"I have made it out for a six-month term," she said. "If you want to stay longer that is great. But I need a six-month minimum term, if that is OK."

"Yes, fine." The man said as he took the paper from her. "Here is the money." He counted the notes from a large bundle of notes in his hand and took her pen, signed the paper and handed it back to her. Audrey took the money and the agreement and left him to explore the property.

CHAPTER 5

Bruce Bromley was curious about his new neighbor. He made an excuse to his wife who was busy mucking about at the bench in the kitchen. "Just going to check on the traps," he said as he made his way out the back door towards the bush track.

"Don't be long," called his wife. "Lunch will be ready in twenty minutes."

Bruce had been feeling his age lately. He had just turned sixty-five and wondered if he would ever experience the excitement he felt in the good old days. His forty-year marriage had left him a hollowed and drained man.

He saw her. Her hair was the color of corn. Her body was strong and straight on a short frame. Dressed all in black. He could feel adrenalin pumping in his veins as he held back the thorny branches of the gorse bush blocking his full view.

She was bending over arranging boxes in the back of a Rav4. He could see the full, rounded shape of her buttocks. Suddenly she stood upright. He panicked and cursed as the thorns of the gorse ripped into his arm. "Bloody Hell" he muttered.

He saw her look over at his hiding place as if she knew he was there. He was too far away and well hidden in the brush. He watched as she grabbed a box and headed down the little concrete path towards her cottage and out of his sight.

Bruce sucked at the newly formed drops of blood and made his way back to the house. He kicked off his gumboots exposing woolly, black, worn socks. His stature was thick and stumpy. His thick black hair was now a long-forgotten memory replaced with a widening bald circle that shone uncomfortably atop his rosy round head. Bruce always wore a moustache. His wife hated it. Said it was like a dead mouse stuck to his upper lip. But then, she didn't like much about him anyway. She slept in her own bedroom at the other end of the house. Said he snored. But he knew it was because she didn't want to be touched anymore which left him with a deep longing and an aching sadness. His wife called from the kitchen "Lunch is on the table." The thought of the lady next door was giving him an appetite. "Coming!" he called.

CHAPTER 6

G avin called his sister to tell her he was moving into the cabin and to thank her for her help. He could tell she was relieved he was not coming back. He immediately began to unpack his few belongings into the tall chest of drawers. He hung his coat in the wardrobe and made his way outside to explore the beach and check out the fishing. It was not a warm day and a cool wind was blowing off the ocean. He would pick up some bait when he went into town for supplies.

The road to the beach went along a grassy high ridge. It was gated at both ends to keep the sheep enclosed. He saw two lambs and two grown sheep at the end of the ridge. They were obviously pet sheep and came running towards him expecting some sort of welcome or food. He gave them neither and shooed them away.

At the end of the ridge the gravel road led down a steep incline towards the ocean. Huge pine trees bordered the road interspersed with manuka (tea tree) and native ferns. He could hear the waves crashing against the rocks, as he got closer to the shore.

It was a beautiful sight. Black rocks with swirling yellow seaweed and clear turquoise water rising and falling like ocean breaths with the incoming tide.

A huge black rock protruded out into the sea. "The perfect fishing spot," said Gavin. *I made a good choice moving here*, he thought as he made his way back up the steep windy road back to the cabin. As he approached the cabin he noticed the sky beginning to darken as grey clouds began to form overhead. "Looks like rain" he said.

CHAPTER 7

Constable Bromley was doing his usual morning rounds. A leisurely drive through the main street of Mangonui took all of five minutes. The small historic resort settlement in the far north of New Zealand comprises of a handful of restaurants, a four-square convenience store, which is also the local bank and post-shop, and a couple of touristy shops struggling now in the winter months as the population shrinks to its mere fifteen hundred residents.

Mangonui means "big shark" derived from the Maori myth of Taniwha who, in the form of a shark, accompanied the canoe, Riukaramea, into the bay. Tucked in the waters of scenic Doubtless Bay it was once a whaling settlement and one of the oldest European settlements in New Zealand. Fittingly named, "Doubtless Bay," when Captain Cook said "Doubtless a bay" after sighting it.

Today, Mangonui is a middle-class town - a little on the upper crust side with comfortably off retirees who play croquet, bridge and bowls at local clubs.

Constable Bromley didn't expect today to be any different

from any other winter day. The wind was howling across the bay causing waves to crash angrily across the narrow street.

A few locals had braved the weather and were taking refuge in the corner coffee shop. A couple waved at him as he passed by. It was a friendly town. Local residents caused no trouble. It was mostly out in the rural areas that required his attention. A few known "P" houses and weed sites were scattered in the surrounding bush areas.

Kaitaia was a different story. A couple of years ago a major drug bust in the city, thirty miles west of Mangonui on the main highway, resulted in hundreds of thousands of methamphetamines being confiscated.

Ten years ago, fifty people were arrested and charged with more than two hundred drug offences. A hundred police officers swooped on forty-two houses in Kaitaia and surrounding areas seizing methamphetamine, cannabis, firearms, vehicles, cash, and drug manufacturing equipment.

Murders were almost commonplace in Kaitaia. However there had not been any significant crime in the quiet town of Mangonui for many years.

Twenty years ago, a twenty-three-year-old girl was found dead in a shallow grave on a farm only four miles south of Mangonui. Her ex-boyfriend was found guilty of the crime and then released seven years later after absence of any physical evidence and his confession being exposed as false. He returned to Mangonui and worked on the fishing boats and rebuilt his house that had burned to the ground while he was in prison. The man's nephew was later suspected as the girl's murderer, but no real evidence resulted in the crime being unsolved to this day.

Constable Bromley took an interest in the history of the area. The notorious Edward Lionel Terry, a White supremacist, in 1905 worked in Mangonui as a surveyor for the Lands and

Survey Department where he wrote "The Shadow" a book of verse with a long introduction on the need for racial purity. Terry, known for his straight posture and magnificent physique, carried out a marathon walk of nearly nine hundred miles from Mangonui to Wellington handing out copies of his book and giving lectures on the yellow peril.

He tried to convince members of the House of Representatives and Immigrations that all non-European immigration should be stopped. With no success he retaliated by shooting Joe Kum Yung on the night of 24th September 1905. Terry told the police upon capture his Book, "The Shadow," would explain his action.

The police station sat perched on a rise at the end of town overlooking a beautiful bay dotted with white, painted terraced houses. His job came complete with a three-bedroom weatherboard house that comfortably housed his wife, his three children and their boxer dog. He worked alone but was in constant contact with the neighboring police stations.

He turned left on the main highway and headed east towards Hihi, a seaside settlement ten minutes down the road. He knew Hihi was pretty deserted in the winter. Apart from the local motor camp and sprinkling of homes it is isolated and remote. The beach area is alcohol free and there is a protected kiwi zoned peninsula past the camp with a handful of year-round residents overlooking the ocean.

As he drove past the beach towards the motor camp he saw a blonde, middle- aged lady at the row of letterboxes outside the campgrounds. He noticed the new green box with a big sign "No junk mail." She had lifted the lid and was peering hopefully inside. He saw her return to her car - a Rav4, badly dented and looking worse for wear. He wondered if she had just moved into the area. He had never seen her before. As he passed her she looked at him and gave him a big smile and a wave. *Friendly lady,* he thought as he smiled back.

He looked in is rear vision mirror and saw she was following him up the peninsula road. He decided he would turn around at the base of the hill and head on back to town. There was nothing happening here and he had a heap of paperwork sitting on his desk that needed attending to. As he turned around, he saw the blonde lady continuing up the peninsula road. There were only a few residents living on the kiwi zone and he wondered which house was hers. *Very isolated for women,* he thought. *I don't suppose she lives alone.* He would ask his uncle next time he saw him if he knew who she was. His Uncle lived on a hundred-acre property up there and seemed to know just about everyone in the Hihi township.

CHAPTER 8

Audrey looked at the time on the bloody noisy kitchen clock. It was almost noon. She had done nothing all morning except stoke the fire and do last night's dishes. Still in her dressing gown with her hair unkempt she peered through the closed curtains at the day. The last couple of days had been wet and dreary. The rain had stopped but the sea was still stormy and rough. Not a boat in sight. She closed the curtains, put another log on the fire and returned to her chaise chair in front of the muted television.

She had a lot on her mind. It was time. She needed to make a plan. She already had the opportunity to check out the new tenant's belongings. Not much to look at; a few clothes, a shaving kit, fishing gear and an old tin box hidden at the back of one of the drawers. It was locked and Audrey could not find the key anywhere. He obviously liked to read. The bedside table had a pile of stacked books, mostly war novels. His life looked a little sad. No photos of family. No personal items. She looked for a computer and was pleased to see he did not own one. *Good*, she thought.

Her thoughts drifted back to the locked tin in the cabin. What the hell is so important that he needs to keep it under lock and key? She wondered where he might keep the key. Her curiosity was getting the better of her. Audrey didn't like secrets unless they were her secrets. She had many secrets but she kept them locked up in her head. She would wait until he went out in his car and then give the cabin a good search.

Audrey's plan was beginning to take form. Today she would check out the cliff to the front beach. Over the past few weeks she had cut out rough clay steps in the bank leading to the rocky shore below. It was a precarious track and could not be seen from either the ocean or from the cottage and cabin. A track through the bush led to the cliff. It was a lot easier going downhill and took only a few minutes to reach the private, secluded, beach below. She knew it would be easy to trip and fall over the bank and, if the tide was in, a body could easily wash out to sea.

Audrey chose her "projects" carefully. They were always middle-aged men specializing in nasty, revolting, sordid, and sickening behavior due to their filthy minds. Narcissistic men who preferred to pay for sex rather than be in a normal healthy relationship. Men whose preference was girls twenty, even thirty years younger than themselves. Men who thought their sexual prowess rendered them superior beings allowing them to treat women as mere pawns in their quest for sexual satisfaction.

All throughout Audrey's life men had poked and prodded their penises in and around her sorry existence. Audrey preferred the soft curves of a feminine body but was not attracted sexually to women. She wished she were. Men were like animals. Prostitution provided sex without foreplay. Gay men, she noticed, didn't bother with foreplay. It was a feminine need. "Bim Bam, thank you Mam" rang in her head making Audrey more and more pissed off.

It had been almost a year since her last project. This time she had to be more careful. More prepared. She had been too reckless before. She couldn't afford to have her name associated anymore with any disappearances.

The noise of a car backing out of the driveway jerked Audrey out of her troubled thoughts. *He is going out, great.* She grabbed the keys and made her way across the soggy grass to the cabin.

CHAPTER 9

Gavin drove carefully down the long tree lined driveway. He wondered if any of the trees actually fell during the strong winds. He sure wouldn't want to be here when that happened. It would be certain death. He reached across the passenger seat and flicked open the lid of his cell phone. He refused to buy an iPhone. No one called him anyway. His phone said it was just after noon. He thought he would spoil himself with a hot feed of fish'n'chips from the Mangonui Fish and Chip shop. While he was in town he would stop off and pick up another book or two from the little local library. There was not much to do in his rented cabin. He was planning on doing some fishing tomorrow if the weather improved and made a mental note to pick up some bait from the Four-Square shop.

The drive to Mangonui took him past the Hihi waterfront. The usual calm blue of the water was now grey and choppy. The waves lapped against the rocky shoreline. The tide was in. It had an almost ominous feel reminding Gavin of when his mother had said it was as if someone was walking over your grave. He shuddered at the thought.

The five-kilometer drive down Hihi road to the Highway was deserted. Olive groves and farmland bordered the rural road. As he hit the main highway the traffic was scarce.

The far north is sparsely populated and Hihi to Taipa is only a nine-kilometer distance. From there it is thirty kilometers to Kaitaia, the furthest northern city in New Zealand. That is if you call a population of under five thousand a city.

Gavin dropped his speed as he entered the small shopping village just a kilometer off the main road. A Thai Restaurant, an Indian restaurant both closed for the winter. Another two fish and chip shops boasting the "best fish." He presumed they offered the locals an alternative to the expensive tourist Fish 'n 'Chip restaurant located on the waterfront.

He pulled in to one of the many empty spaces in front of the restaurant. He was surprised to see it was remarkably busy considering the weather. He put in his order, purchased a beer from the bar and made his way over to the wooden benches. His number was sixty-six.

They said they would call out the number when it was ready. He looked around at his fellow patrons. Middle aged couples, elderly couples and a few obvious foreigners. You could tell they were foreigners from their dress. German, Swiss – he couldn't tell which.

He gazed out the large glass windows to the boats anchored in the bay. They were bobbing up and down in the winter swell. Gavin pulled a newspaper from his coat pocket and started to read.

"Prostitution in the Far North -The Far North District Council had brought in a new bylaw restricting where brothels can open - The by-law, which came into effect on February 1, 2005, prevents brothels from operating within 100 meters of schools, kindergartens, childcare centers and churches. The bylaw was

necessary under the Prostitution Reform Act. However, small owner-operated establishments, with up to four sex workers operating individually, are exempt from the location restrictions.

He continued to read about a situation in the far north where young girls are working outside the law – offering sex for money under the legal age of eighteen.

Gavin liked young girls. The younger - the better. He wondered where these girls were operating. Tonight, he would make a trip up and down the main highway between Mangonui and Kaitaia and see if he could get lucky. The cabin was the ideal spot for a bit of hanky panky and he smiled as he remembered he had everything he needed. He patted the key in his trouser pocket and smiled. Things were looking up.

CHAPTER 10

Constable Bromley looked at the email that had just arrived on his laptop. "Damn" he cursed. He knew tonight was going to be a busy night. The Kaitaia police were doing a sting on local prostitutes. Even though prostitution was legal in New Zealand, there were strict rules on age limits and locations. He knew the city of Whangarei, two hours south of Mangonui, had a legal brothel with about twelve sex workers. There were no brothels in the far north as local Churches opposed the practice with a fury. Now, with the influx of young girls thought to be between fifteen and seventeen working the streets, complaints had been made to the local police demanding they put a stop to it. Constable Bromley emailed them back to say he would do a sweep of his areas between eleven and three a.m. from Hihi to Taipa. He hoped they would be satisfied with that.

He looked out the window at the waterfront. The weather was blustery and wintery. Rain was expected this evening. It was going to be a long day and a long night. He noticed a silver

Toyota Celica pull into the parking area in front of the fish and chip shop. He watched as a tall, lean man stepped out of the car and walked quickly into the restaurant. He had not seen him before. He didn't look like a tourist. His car was not a rental car, it looked too old and worn. He wondered if he had a new resident in his area. Or maybe he was just passing through. He went back to the paperwork on his desk.

The phone rang. It was his uncle from Hihi.

"Jimmy" he heard his name booming down the line. "What's up?"

"Nothing much" said Constable Bromley pleased to have a distraction from his paperwork. "What's up with you"?

"Would you like to come over tonight – bring Mary and the kids? Haven't seen you in ages and Marge is cooking a roast lamb."

"Sorry," said Bromley "Can't tonight - been called in on a job. Will be working till the wee hours of the morning. Another night."

"Sure, understand old boy. Another time."

Constable Bromley knew his uncle was disappointed. They were a close family. "By the way" he asked. "Do you know if a blonde lady in her fifties has moved in up your way? I saw her at the letterboxes. I didn't know any property was purchased up there."

"You are pretty on to it," said his uncle. "Yes, she has moved in next door. It is her family's land I understand. They live overseas. She has been cleaning it up, cutting down trees, renovating the buildings and so forth. Making a good job, I hear. Why do you ask?"

"Oh, nothing really," said the constable. "Just didn't recognize her – is she living alone up there?"

"I think so," said his uncle. "Pretty isolated up here. Maybe I should go over and check on her. Be neighborly and so on. Let's get together next week some time. Marge misses your kids now our grandchildren are living in Australia, they are all she has to fuss over."

"That would be great," said the Constable.

CHAPTER 11

Bruce Bromley hung up the phone and felt elated. Now he had an excuse to meet his blonde buxom neighbor. He told his wife Jimmy couldn't make it tonight. She was obviously disappointed. Now she had to spend the evening in his company and he knew she was tiring of their situation. This was their dream home they have saved for their whole married life. But the reality of living in isolation away from their children and grandchildren was not in their plans. They hoped they would spend more time visiting them. But now they had moved to work in Australia and life was proving lonely for Marge. Bruce had his possum, stoat and weasel trapping. They also had their boat that had not been used in months. Marge didn't like fishing and Bruce preferred company on his boat.

It was a shame Jimmy and the kids could not make it tonight. Tomorrow Bruce would make his way over to meet his neighbor. He didn't want to tell his wife. She would want to bake a cake or bread or some other silly thing to welcome her. He wanted to keep this lady all to himself. Marge needn't know about her.

Bruce looked in the mirror and patted his hair on both sides of his balding head. He smiled to expose his worn teeth. "Not too bad" he said in complete denial "I don't look a day over fifty –five." He made his way into the kitchen to make a cup of coffee and read the local paper. He read about the young girl prostitutes and how the local church was demanding the police put a stop to under aged prostitution. Bruce had never paid for sex and never understood why any man would need to. He much preferred a real relationship with a woman. Now the lady next door would do him just fine.

"What did Jimmy have to say?" asked his wife sitting down at the table across from him.

"Said he had to work tonight. Didn't say what he was working on. Just said he had to work until the wee hours of the morning."

"Must be working on the stink about those young girls walking the streets," said Marge. "Awful isn't it? I wonder what their parents are thinking - letting them wander the streets at all hours. They should be at home doing their homework. They must still be in high school. What is the world coming to?" Marge picked up a page of the paper and started reading. "We should join the local bridge club," she said. "We need to get out more."

CHAPTER 12

"Shit, Shit, Shit." Audrey was pissed off. She had looked through everything in the cabin but couldn't find the key to the box. She shook the box and it sounded like metal objects inside. She knew she couldn't stay in the cabin too long. He might come back at any moment. She returned to her cottage feeling completely deflated. She hated not knowing what he might have to hide. *He must carry the key on him*, she thought. Which meant she was out of luck.

She pulled the lawn mower out from under the cabin and began to mow the lawns. Audrey took pride in the properties she looked after. It was supposed to rain again tonight and she may as well mow the lawns before her tenant returned. The lawnmower was noisy and the wind was howling. The weather suited her mood. She must be patient. As always, situations seemed to sort themselves out. She would find out what her tenants secrets were, and if he deserved to be her next project. She suspected that he did. Most men did.

It was late afternoon before he returned to the cabin. Audrey peered through her curtains and watched him remove the keys from his trouser pocket and open up the sliding door. She was sure the key to his box was on the same ring. She couldn't see him once he went inside. She wondered where he put the keys. All she had to do was to separate him from his keys. It wouldn't be easy.

Once Audrey obsessed over something she couldn't let it go. The bloody box was becoming just that. A nice hot bath and a glass of wine would relax her. She turned on the hot tap and watched as the boiling hot water hissed and spat in fury. She had a wetback fireplace and Audrey kept the fire lit every day to heat the water. In the winter, the fire was lit both day and night and the water reached boiling point. Sometimes Audrey had to have two baths a day to release the boiling hot water in the cylinder. Rainwater was collected on the roof and ran into the two large tanks behind the cabin. Water from the heavens, pure and clean. It has been a dry winter up until now and the rain tonight would be a welcome sight.

It was primitive living. The cottage was originally an old tin garage. The plumbing, septic and drainage were all in need of repair. Fifty years ago the cottage and land were given to the care-taker of the large farm that covered the peninsula. Today the peninsula was covered in bush and subdivided into private properties, recently becoming a protective kiwi zone.

Audrey's property was the closest to the Hihi public beach and unfortunately her two private beaches were accessible to the public when the tide was out. Occasionally she found fishermen fishing off the large rock at one of her beaches. The other beach was much more private requiring people to clamber over huge craggy rocks to access the beach area. This was the beach she had made accessible by cutting steps into the cliff.

The cabin was a more recent addition. The last owners had erected the small unit. It was also in desperate need of a face-lift when Audrey moved in. Now it was presentable and even comfortable and thank goodness provided her with a much-needed income.

Audrey leaned back in the bath and sipped her wine. She played Mozart on her computer. She had copied over three thousand songs from her CDs left at the Three Suites. Now they were all on iTunes. The music calmed her mind and the hot water calmed her body. She heard the phone ring and ignored it. There was no one she wanted to talk to.

CHAPTER 13

Suzy was getting ready for her night out. She had told her parents she was staying at Lucy's house. Lucy had told her parents the same thing – that is, she was staying at Suzy's house.

Together they had arranged to meet up with Staci, who Suzy had met at the summer camp. Suzy looked at her reflection in the full-length mirror. She looked older than her sixteen years. Especially when she put on makeup and fluffed her long red hair out so it looked sexy and full. She had a pale complexion. She knew men liked her pale skin and red hair. Her big green eyes and full red lips made up for her lack of experience in the sex world. Staci was older and more experienced.

This was Suzy's fifth time out. It was Lucy's first time. Suzy stuffed her work clothes and makeup bag into her backpack and went to kiss her parents goodbye. Lucy's house was just down the next street. She was actually meeting Lucy outside the old library. They were planning on going to the movies in Kaitaia before hitting the streets later that night. Staci was going to take them to work in the small town of Taipa. There had been a lot of trouble lately with under aged sex workers and they heard that the Kaitaia cops would be checking the city streets tonight so working out of town was their only option.

After the movie, the girls changed their youthful faces into desirable women with mascara, lipstick and powders. Their jeans and sweaters were replaced with short skirts, knee-high boots, push up bras and leather jackets. Lucy had to borrow Suzy's clothes as her parents were strict and conservative unlike Suzy's Mum and Dad, who pretty much let Suzy wear what she wanted. They reviewed their metamorphosis with giggling delight. They could hear it was beginning to rain. They hoped they would get picked up early and taken somewhere nice and warm.

Staci dropped them off under cover at the small shopping center on the main highway out of town. The shops were closed and they huddled together under the awning.

It wasn't long before a man in a red truck stopped and asked Lucy if she would like to go somewhere for a 'good time.' Lucy was pleased she was chosen over Suzy and eagerly got in his truck leaving Suzy alone in the cold wet night.

Suzy began to regret her decision to work tonight. Twice she had to crouch down on the wet pavement behind a bench to hide from a police car cruising the area. Luckily she spotted the well-marked car in time. Staci hadn't told them the police would be cruising Taipa too. She must be careful.

It was after midnight when she saw the man pull into the shopping center. He was a rather good-looking, older man and spoke in a soft, well-educated voice.

"Hello there. What is a nice looking girl doing out here in the middle of no-where on such a cold night."

"Looking for a good time," she replied bravely.

"I can provide that," he said. "Hop in."

"It will cost you a hundred bucks" she said and waited for his response.

"No problem, hundred dollars it is," he said as he leaned over to open the passenger door for her.

Suzy noticed the interior of the car was clean and tidy. "Where are we going?" she asked.

"To a nice warm cabin" he replied. "About twenty minutes from here. How much for the whole night?" he asked.

Suzy thought for a moment. She had her cell phone on her and could text Staci later to let her know she would not be back until tomorrow morning. "Five hundred bucks" she said boldly.

"Make it three hundred and we have a deal," he said.

Suzy thought about it. Three hundred bucks and a warm place to hang out sounded OK to her.

"It's a deal," she said and sat quietly beside him as they made their way through the dark night.

CHAPTER 14

Constable Bromley had cruised the area for more than three hours. Nothing. He doubted anyone would be working on such a wet, cold night. He had only passed a couple of cars and that was a couple of hours ago. One looked like the silver Toyota that belonged the man at the fish and chip shop in Mangonui this afternoon. He wondered what he was doing out so late. He could see someone in the car with him – but who? He couldn't see clearly in the rain – it was too dark and wet. *He must be staying locally*, he thought.

Bromley looked at the time. Almost two o'clock in the morning. He made his way back to the station. What a waste of an evening. He could have been eating a nice roast lamb dinner by a warm fireplace with his family. Instead he was out looking for wayward girls selling their bodies for a few bucks. His oldest daughter was sixteen. She was a good girl - never any trouble. He didn't know what sort of parents would let their children walk the streets.

He was told that legalizing prostitution cleaned up the business. It was the oldest profession in the world. Personally, he thought prostitution should be illegal and smoking weed should be legal. California and Colorado legalized marijuana. He knew prostitution was illegal over there. New Zealand had it all wrong he thought. Maybe methamphetamines would not be such a problem in New Zealand if weed was legal. But who was he to complain. He had a job to do.

As soon as he had filled out his paperwork he made his way over to his house next door. It was another night of creeping into bed so not to disturb his sleeping wife. He was asleep before his head hit the pillow.

CHAPTER 15

G avin parked on the gravel drive about thirty feet from the cabin. He didn't want to wake Audrey next door. The rain had stopped long enough for them both to make their way inside.

He turned on the television to a music channel and opened up a bottle of wine. He passed one glass to Suzy who had removed her wet jacket and muddy boots and was warming her exposed legs by the electric panel heater. She looked a little bedraggled he thought. Her long red hair was dripping at the ends making small puddles on the floor. Her eye makeup made black, raccoon-like circles around her pretty green eyes. Gavin didn't mind. He realized he had struck it lucky. She was much younger than he had first thought. He could tell she was only about sixteen or seventeen.

"What sort of music do you like?" he asked pleasantly.

"Oh, most anything" she replied.

He kept it on the groove channel but he guessed she would have preferred one of Justin Beiber's songs. He watched as she confidently sipped her glass of wine and was surprised at her obvious sophistication and her lack of concern at being in a stranger's isolated cabin in the middle of the night. *She must have been doing this for some time*, he thought.

"I need the money first," Suzy said pouting her beautiful full lips provocatively.

Gavin picked up his keys and walked toward the chest of drawers. He reached into the back of the second drawer and removed a metal box and placed it on the small wooden kitchen table.

Suzy looked intently as he unlocked the box and lifted the lid. She couldn't see what was inside but was pleased to see he had a wad of money in his hand. He removed three crisp hundred-dollar notes and returned the wad to the box. "Three hundred" he said as he handed her the money.

"Thanks," said Suzy and tucked the money into her wet boot on the floor. "Now what would you like?" she asked as she stood facing the older, good-looking man.

"This" he said as he pulled out a small black cotton blindfold from the box and proceeded to tie it around her pretty head. "Don't worry," he said. "I won't hurt you. It is just a game." He led her to the bed and pulled her gently down onto the fresh clean duvet. He rested her head on the pillow and began to slowly undress her. She lay quietly and obediently still. He prized open her young legs and touched her in places that made her sigh. Suzy liked older men. She liked the way they smelt. His soft scent of aftershave and musty body door reminded her of her first time she had sex with an older man. It was during the summer holidays just a few months ago. He was staying at the same camping grounds as her family. He was married with children her age. They would meet in the bush down an isolated track most afternoons. He taught her about her body and how good it felt to be touched. They made love in the sunshine. It was at the summer camp that she also met Staci and learned she could make money doing the same thing. She loved it. She knew she looked mature for her age and men would pay good money to be with her and she wasn't wrong. Her dream was to be a porn star like the ones she saw on television. She only had a few years to wait before she could open up her own brothel. By then she should have enough money. Tonight she was making three hundred dollars and as long she was back home in the morning her parents would never know. Little did she know her choice of tonight's sugar daddy was not a good one.

CHAPTER 16

udrey couldn't stand it. She had heard his car return about twelve thirty. She wondered why he had parked so far down the driveway. She heard the little metal gate to the cabin clink shut and footsteps going into the cabin. Soft music began to play. Audrey had to strain to hear. She thought she heard voices but a new shower of deafening rain and high winds made it impossible to eavesdrop. Looking out the curtains didn't provide any more information. His curtains were drawn and his lights were low. She would have to wait until morning.

The weather forecast on the late news had forecasted more showers tomorrow turning into heavy rain in the evening. She turned down the fire and switched off the lights and climbed into bed. Tonight she would sleep with the electric blanket on two. She reached over to take a couple of sleeping pills and a sip of water. Tomorrow she would do some serious snooping. Audrey drifted off to sleep with visions of metal boxes and dark places.

CHAPTER 17

Constable Bromley slept in late. His late night of cruising the streets in the rain had been uneventful and he was in no hurry to venture out into the heavy rain. He could hear pounding on the tin roof. Mary had been kind enough to let him sleep in. She was in the kitchen with the three girls. He was pleased to hear his older daughter's voice. He didn't like her staying away at night. His stomach let him know he hadn't eaten a meal in too long. Bacon, eggs and cooked tomatoes would go down really well right now. He swung his legs over the bed and pulled on a pair of sweatpants. Work could wait another few hours.

Bromley was pleased with his body. He kept himself fit and healthy. You never knew when you needed to run down a young hoodlum. He knew he could outrun almost anyone even though he was turning forty-five this week. Daily runs and weightlifting were two of his favorite hobbies. His thirty-three-inch waist had never altered since his high school days. He knew his wife was pleased he looked after himself. Their friends were beginning to let themselves go. He was proud of how Mary still had kept her youthful body. She didn't look a year over thirty-five. Their daughters had taken after her. They were pretty, petite and athletic. He was proud of his family.

He heard the phone ringing in the kitchen.

"Hello, Mary speaking" he heard his wife singing into the phone. "It's for you," she said as she handed him the phone.

"Constable Bromley, how can I help you?" he asked grudgingly hoping the call would not take him away from his pending breakfast. "No, she is not here." He said looking across at his daughter, Lucy. "Lucy have you seen Suzy this morning? Her parents say she didn't come home this morning. I thought you were staying at her house last night?"

Lucy looked concerned. "No, we went to the movies and then I decided to come home afterwards. Last time I saw her was when we said goodbye after the movies."

Bromley repeated the information to the concerned parents. He looked over at Lucy again "Her parents said she was staying here with you last night and she hasn't come home yet."

Lucy just shrugged her shoulders and returned to eating her cornflakes. "Maybe she is with Staci," she said quietly.

"Staci who?" he asked.

"She's Suzy's friend. She met her at summer camp," mumbled Lucy almost incoherently. "She lives in Taipa down by the recycling place. She came to the movies with us in Kaitaia."

By the time Bromley had hung up the phone from Suzy's parents he knew breakfast would have to wait. They had never heard of Suzy's so-called friend, Staci. Bromley promised to drive down to the recycling area and question the handful of residents who lived nearby. He was sure there was no need for concern. He had told Suzy's parents that Suzy had most probably just spent the night with this Staci and didn't want to concern them with her change of plans.

The drive to Taipa was not an easy one. The streets were strewn with branches and debris from last night's storm. Twice he had to stop to remove large branches from the road. The rain had not let up since last night. He made his way across the one-way bridge and turned left down the deserted road along the Taipa River to the recycling depot. He chose the yellow house set back from the road, parked his car and walked up the wooden steps to the front door.

A quick sharp knock brought a woman to the door. "I am looking for a girl called Staci," said Bromley.

"She lives next door," said the women pointing to the old farmhouse across the grassy paddocks separating their two properties.

"Thanks, said Bromley, "sorry to disturb you."

He returned to the car and set off back down the road to the house the lady had pointed out. He heard a dog barking loudly inside the house. He knocked equally loudly on the door. It took a minute or two before he heard footsteps approaching. When the door opened he looked into the eyes of a beautiful young women. He guessed she was about eighteen years old. She was impeccably dressed.

"Would you be Staci?" he asked.

"Yes." She replied looking at him defiantly.

"Were you with a girl called Suzy last night?" he asked her.

"Yes" she replied again.

"Is she here? Did she stay here last night?" he pushed further hoping to get a longer response.

"No" she replied noncommittally.

"Do you know where she is? Her parents are worried. She never returned home last night."

"I thought she was staying with her friend, Lucy," said Staci. "You can check with her. She lives in Mangonui I think."

"No, she did not stay with Lucy," said Bromley not divulging the fact that Lucy was his daughter. "Do you know any other friend she could have stayed with?" he asked.

"No" replied Staci "Sorry I can't help you officer. Is there anything else?" she asked with her hand on the door, in anticipation of closure.

"Not at the moment," said the constable. "Please let me know if you hear from her," he said as he handed her his card, and stepped away from the door and returned to his car.

Something was troubling Bromley. It wasn't just the fact that Suzy was a friend of Lucy and was missing but it was the confusion of why the girls had changed plans and not stayed overnight where they said they were staying. Suzy's parents thought Suzy was staying with Lucy and Lucy had told him she was staying at Suzy's house. Yet Lucy came home and now Suzy was nowhere to be found. He made his way over to Suzy's house to talk to her parents. He wondered. Did Suzy have a cell phone? When was the last time they had talked to her? He had his work cut out for him. He would stop by the coffee shop and pick up a steak and cheese pie and a cup of coffee. He needed food so he could think clearly.

CHAPTER 18

Audrey awoke late and noticed Gavin's car was already gone. "Damn," she said. "I missed him" wondering if she had time to have another look for the key to box in the cabin. She threw on a pair of jeans and a warm sweatshirt, grabbed the umbrella and made her way across the square concrete stepping-stones between the two buildings. She listened intently through the wind and rain in case she heard his car coming up the driveway.

Carefully wiping her wet shoes she stepped inside and was shocked at the sight before her. The cabin was a mess. Everything was in disarray. The bed linens, pillows and clothes were strewn everywhere. The drawer where the box was kept was left open. She noticed the tin box was now sitting on the kitchen table. It was empty. The lid was open and the key was in the lock.

She picked up the duvet from the floor and a pair of women's panties fell out and landed on her shoe. "Oh shit!" she quickly kicked them off. "What the hell?" Was Gavin wearing women's underwear? She noticed they had little pink and purple scattered hearts with a pink lace trim. They looked more like a young girl's panties. Did he have a girl here? She thought she heard voices last night. Where were they now? It was dangerous driving around in this weather. Trees were already swaying precariously in the violent storm.

She didn't dare to clean anything up. He would know she had been inside the cabin. Snooping around was one thing but it looked as though there was a struggle here. Something untoward had gone on and she would find out just what it was. In the meantime better leave everything as it was. She replaced the duvet onto the floor, tore off a paper towel from the roll on the counter and wrapped the panties inside. She would keep the panties until she found out what had been going on here. If he was indeed a child molester, she had her next project confirmed. She looked around the room, dusted off any area she had touched, including the metal box, and quickly left the scene.

CHAPTER 19

Lucy watched her father leave through the front door. "Shit, shit, shit" was all she could think. Where the hell was Suzy? She was just fine when she left her at the shopping center. Lucy checked her phone for the hundredth time. There was a new message. It was from Staci. "*Where the fuck is Suzy!*" she read, "*Call me.*" Lucy went into her bedroom and shut the door to make the call. Staci answered and sounded really pissed off.

"I knew I shouldn't have taken you two last night," she said. "I had a bloody cop come by a few minutes ago asking where Suzy was and if I'd seen her."

"What cop?" Lucy asked already knowing the answer.

"Oh, I dunno... he gave me his card and said to call him if I heard from her. Yeah right! I'm going to call a cop!"

Lucy felt sick. Her father was obviously now involved and if he found out she had been working with Suzy last night she would be in deep shit. Worse still. What if something had happened to Suzy?

"Anyway," Staci added, "Suzy texted me really early this morning to say she was on an overnight job and would find her own way home. Lucky her! She must have made a mint."

Lucy breathed a sigh of relief. Suzy was OK. She would be home soon. Her phone rang again. It was Suzy's Mother. She wanted to know what time they had left the movie theatre. Lucy told her about ten-forty five p.m. and suggested she may have stayed at another friend's house and promised to call around and see if she could find her. All she had to do was to fill in time until Suzy got home. Thank God her Dad would never find out. One thing was for sure; she would never, ever go out on a job with them again.

She had been proud of herself last night. The man who picked her up from Taipa lived on a nearby farm. He had driven her to an old shed on the farm. Said it was his worker's cottage. It had a couple of bunk beds and an old fireplace. The sheets and blankets smelt of stale cows' milk. The floor just had thin wooden slats and the cold air whistled through the gaps.

This was not Lucy's first-time having sex. She had a boyfriend when she was twelve. He was sixteen. Lucy liked having sex. This man was about the same age as her father. She presumed he was married and had his own children. He had wanted straight sex, which was OK with her. She was worried she would get a guy that wanted something kinky. Staci had given her a condom, which the man needed convincing to use. She said she wouldn't do it without it, so he had no choice.

Afterwards he drove her back to where he had picked her up. She had called Staci to collect her and drive her home as it was raining hard and there was no sign of Suzy and she was not answering her phone. It was about half past one when Lucy crept back into her house and into bed. She noticed her father's cop car wasn't outside the station. He was still out working. Now she realized he must have been cruising the area. *Thank God, he hadn't seen them.* Lucy had tucked the crisp hundred-dollar note into her diary. She knew she would never write about last night. Last night was best forgotten.

CHAPTER 20

G avin hadn't meant to kill the girl. They seemed to be having so much fun. She had been OK when he blind folded her and cuffed her hands behind her back. He had talked so softly in her ear saying sweet things and stroking her long slender legs as he pried them open gently and tied them to each side of the bed. She seemed to be turned on by the bondage. He had stroked her thighs, removed her panties, and caressed her sweet pussy. She writhed with pleasure when he licked her there and pinched her sweet young nipples. She was so wet and he was so hard. He came in her more than once. She begged for him to use a condom. Said it was in her backpack and could he go get it. Gavin never used a condom. "Like taking a shower with your clothes on," he would say.

He had stood back and looked at the beautiful naked body on the bed. Perfect in every way. He took his digital camera out of the metal box and started taking photos. She could hear the click of the camera and pleaded with him not to take any photos. Staci had told her over and over again. No photos! No Photos ever!

Gavin took no notice of her pleads. He kept clicking photos while she struggled to loosen the ropes from her legs. She started to panic. Twisting from side to side. The handcuffs made it impossible to remove the blindfold.

Gavin liked the violent moves she was making. It turned him on. Once more he climbed on top of her. He felt his hard penis enter her as he held his hand over her mouth to keep her quiet. It took longer this time to come but it was better than before. He knew he should keep her quiet until he could decide what to do with her.

Gavin was worried Audrey would hear her fretful protests. He took a small white facecloth from the bathroom and made a makeshift gag. She struggled violently as he stuffed the cloth into her mouth.

Her white skin glowed in the darkness of the room. Gavin had turned off all the lights except for the small table lamp by the bed. The glow enabled him to see just enough to collect all the girl's clothing and stuff them into her backpack. He knew he must dispose of everything before morning. Including the girl.

CHAPTER 21

Staci realized it was time to leave. Her suitcase was packed and ready to go. She had called a friend in Whangarei, two hours away and said she needed a place to stay for the next few days. It was easier to just disappear. She didn't want the cops digging into her life. She had been a working girl since she was thirteen. It was all she knew. She had street smarts and had a nice nest egg stacked away for a rainy day. It looked as though that rainy day had come.

The farmhouse she had been staying in belonged to her cousin. He was due back any day now anyway. She would leave a note thanking him for the digs and promising to call when she had settled into her new place in Dunedin. She didn't know why she had said Dunedin. It was not only in the South Island but almost as south as you can get. She didn't know anyone there and seemed liked a good way to mislead the cops. Not that she had anything to hide. Prostitution was legal in New Zealand if you were over eighteen years of age. Staci had just turned eighteen a few months ago and figured she could now work in a brothel - which was a lot safer than on the streets.

Whangarei had a reputable brothel and she would check out the scene there. She didn't think the girl, Suzy, was in any trouble. She had begged and begged Staci to set her up with work. Staci knew it was a stupid thing to do and it could bite her in the ass. And it had.

CHAPTER 22

Constable Bromley knocked at the door of Suzy's parents, Mark and Betty Cunningham. He and his wife had met them briefly at a local farmers' market about a year before. Taipa had a great market on Saturdays. His wife liked to pick up plum sauce and apple and plum chutney from the market. He seldom went to the farmers' market but wanted to spend some quality time with Mary on the weekends. She loved the local scene. The area was known for its olive orchards and local olive oil was proudly sold at the stalls. Fresh bread and preserves, home -made candles, arts and crafts, greenstone jewelry was all on display. Locals played guitars and soft folk music wafted through the school grounds where the market was held.

Mark Cunningham opened the door. He looked worried and quickly invited Bromley inside. Betty, his wife, was on the phone. He could hear her from the next room.

"I just don't know what has got into her" he heard her say. "She always calls home. We haven't heard from her since early last night – it was about six o'clock when she left."

Mark asked Constable Bromley if he had tracked down the Staci girl.

"I talked to her just before I came over here. She said she thought Suzy was staying with Lucy at our house. All rather confusing, I'm sure. She may have stayed at another friend's house and will be back before you know it."

"Betty has called everyone she knows. No one has seen her or heard from her," said Mark. "We have left numerous messages on her cell phone and tried calling her. She isn't answering. We are very worried. What if something has happened to her?"

"I am sure she is just fine," comforted Bromley. "If she is not back by this evening we can put out a missing person bulletin."

"What clothes was she wearing when you last saw her?" He directed to Betty as she entered the room.

"Jeans, pink sweater, navy jacket and white Reeboks and she was carrying her blue backpack. It has a pink stripe on it." Betty replied tearfully.

"Do you have a current photo you can email me?" asked Bromley handing Betty his card. "Please, I wouldn't worry. I am sure she will be back soon. Call me if you hear anything."

Mark walked to the door with Bromley. "Suzy is a lovely girl," he said. "She has never caused any problems. I am worried about her. She should have been back by now."

Constable Bromley was also concerned. As he returned to his car he was still puzzled as to why Lucy had Suzy had parted ways last night after the movies. He would talk to Lucy again and get to the bottom of it. Before he could do that he needed to get the paperwork underway and put out a bulletin to the other stations.

CHAPTER 23

Audrey looked at the girl's panties with distaste. She was careful not to touch them. His DNA would come in handy. She would need to make some mental adjustments to her plan but it was nothing she couldn't handle.

His car made crunching sounds on the gravel as it approached the cabin. He parked outside the cabin gate and made his way quickly inside. Audrey noticed he looked extremely distraught. He was wearing gumboots and carrying a large bag. She looked at the small alarm clock on her bedside table. It was just after mid-day. She hoped he would clean up the mess he had made in the cabin. It wasn't a day to work outside. The wind and rain were constant. She turned on the television and checked out the latest movies on her Apple TV. *All in good time*, she thought.

The knock at the door startled her. Living in such isolation created an unconscious fear of intrusion by others. She looked in the wall mirror and decided there was nothing she could do to improve her image in an instant. Bravely she approached the sliding glass doors to the patio. A man stood there - balding, short and stocky. He was beaming exposing large teeth and tight lips.

"Sorry to disturb you," he said. "I am Bruce Bromley, your neighbor next door. Just wanted to say hello and introduce myself."

Audrey was annoyed. She hated neighbors and hated friendly, chatty, nosey neighbors even more.

"Pleased to meet you" she said. "I am Audrey."

"I didn't know this property was for sale," he said. "Are you the new owner?"

"This property belongs to my family. I am just making renovations and clearing the land for them." She gave him a big smile and said," I am so sorry, I would invite you in for a cup of tea but I am just about to go out. I have an appointment in town. Thanks for stopping by. It is a pleasure meeting you."

The man looked disappointed as Audrey reached for her coat and hat.

"Oh, no worries" he said. "I'll be on my way. You know where to find me if you should need anything."

Audrey watched him walking up the driveway. He had not come in a car or she would have heard it. He must have walked over. It was quite a distance from his property to hers. Maybe he has a track through the bush. She would check it out. She didn't want anyone keeping an eye on her. That was the last thing she needed. She returned her hat and coat to the clothes rack by the door and went back to her movie. Bloody neighbors.

CHAPTER 24

Bruce was disappointed to say the least. He had been looking forward to meeting his new neighbor and had changed into his good jeans and best winter jacket for the occasion. He had not told Marge he was going out. She had left an hour ago to meet up with her friends at the bowling club. He had walked down the wide grass track between the two properties. It was a track made by the installation of the old concrete water tanks over forty years ago. The track could not be seen from Audrey's property. He guessed she didn't know the track even existed and he wouldn't divulge the information.

Audrey. He liked the name. It suited her. He liked her smile too. He just wished he had more time to get to know her. This was one friend he would keep to himself. No need for his wife to get involved. He made his way back down the track to the house. The wind was getting stronger. He watched as the trees swayed precariously. Large drops of rain began to fall making his retreat seem even more depressing. He pulled up the collar of his jacket and walked more briskly.

As soon as Bruce had taken off his wet clothes and changed

into his favorite old jeans and woolly jumper he picked up the phone and called Jimmy.

Jimmy picked up immediately and sounded distracted "Mangonui Police station, Constable Bromley speaking. How can I help you?"

"Hey, Jimmy," said Bruce. Sorry to disturb you. You sound busy."

"I am" he replied. "I am on a new case."

"Oh, what sort of case? Asked Bruce.

"Missing girl. Been missing since last night. She is a friend of Lucy's. Damn nice girl. Suzy Cunningham. Do you know her parents? Mark and Mary Cunningham. Nice folks. Live not far from here."

"No, can't say I do. I'll leave you to it. Just called to say I met Audrey from next door. Didn't learn anything new. She said the property belongs to her family and is doing renovations there. Didn't get a chance to find out more." He paused. "Oh, by the way, there appears to be someone living on the property with her. I saw a car parked outside the cabin so I guess she is not alone there. A good thing too. Not a place for a lady on her own."

Bruce hung up the phone and made himself a nice hot cup of tea and sat down in his favorite chair by the window. He never tired of looking at the vast views across the bay and out to sea. He wished the weather would improve and he could take the boat out and do some fishing. Maybe Audrey would like a trip out on the bay. He must ask her.

CHAPTER 25

Gavin didn't waste any time in cleaning up the cabin. The last thing he needed was his landlady seeing what a mess he had got it into. He made the bed and dusted off any fingerprints the girl may have left. He washed the glasses and threw the empty wine bottle into the rubbish tin. He returned the empty tin box to the back of the dresser drawer.

The morning had been a disaster. Everything that could have gone wrong did. It was just after three in the morning when he put the girl and her belongings into the back seat of his Toyota. Not knowing the area made it difficult to navigate the streets in the dark, stormy night. Finally, he made the decision to drop the girl where he had picked her up. He made his way into the deserted shopping area and the small car park facing the main street. He made sure no one was around. The streets were deserted.

He opened the back door and pulled the girl out and put her back where he had found her the night before. He placed the backpack next to her. Then, he had the most dreadful thought. "DNA" he muttered. "Fuck! Why didn't I wear a condom?"

He knew that if the girl was found they would have his DNA. What if someone had seen his car when he picked her up last night? He needed to dispose of the body. Quickly he returned the girl and her belongings back into the car and left the car park heading for the beach.

In a mindless panic he drove around for what seemed hours with the girl lying on the back seat. The rain pounded on the windshield. The wind was howling. His mind was constantly racing. In desperation he decided to take her back to the cabin and hide her in the bush on the property. He had noticed a large, wooded area not far from the driveway. He would have to carry her through the bush, but it was far enough away from the buildings and remote enough for a temporary hiding place. Later he would move her to a safer location.

He parked the Toyota on the driveway just beyond the front wooden gate and carried the girl over his shoulder into the dense bush. It was muddy and slippery and rain and wind made it difficult to maneuver in the dark night. He was grateful for his raincoat, head torch and gumboots.

Finally, he found a hollow in the ground. He dropped the girl and her bag into the shallow grave and covered her with palm fronds and fallen branches. He scooped leaves and pine needles over the body and hoped he had chosen her temporary resting place wisely.

As he made his way back to the car he cursed his stupidity. Why couldn't he have just had a pleasant night with the girl? All was going so well. They were both having a good time. Why did he have to lose it? She was such a pretty girl with all that red hair.

He looked at the clock in the car. Five Thirty. It was almost dawn. He needed time to clear his head and instead of returning to the cabin he backed down out of the driveway and headed off towards the main highway. It took him all morning to find a suitable place to hide the body. He would have to wait until dark before he could risk moving her. In the meantime, he would get some sleep.

CHAPTER 26

L ucy heard her father come home. She knew she was in deep trouble. No one had heard from Suzy since last night. She was missing and it was all her fault. She should have waited for her to return instead of coming home. If her father ever found out that she was 'working' last night, he would kill her. "Stupid, stupid, idiot," she cursed at herself "Why did I do it? All for a measly hundred bucks."

She heard the knock on her closed bedroom door. "Lucy?"

It was her father. "Yes," she replied.

He sat on her bed facing her. Lucy was seated at her computer. "We need to talk about last night," her father said seriously. "I want you to go through everything you remember starting from when you left the house."

Lucy's mind froze. She didn't have a good reason for leaving Suzy and she knew her Father wouldn't accept her previous explanation. She needed a new story. One that was half true and more believable.

"I didn't want to say anything before" she started. "But, after the movies Staci dropped Suzy off at the Taipa shopping center.

Suzy said she was meeting a boy there. I don't know what boy she was talking about. She told us not to wait around. It was about eleven fifteen when we dropped her off. I am sorry, Dad, I should have told you before but I didn't want to get Suzy into trouble. If her parents found out she was meeting up with a boy in the middle of the night she would be in awful trouble."

Constable Bromley looked at his daughter. She looked devastated. He could tell she was terribly upset over Suzy's disappearance. "You should never have left Suzy alone in the middle of the night even if she asked you to," he said. "Anything could have happened to her. Staci should have known better. "Is there anything else you should tell me?" he asked.

"No" Lucy replied wiping back her tears. "I am so sorry Dad. It is all my fault she is missing."

Bromley put his arm around his daughter, "We will find her," he said "May this be a lesson for you. You must tell us where you are going when you leave the house. No more secrets, OK?"

"I promise," said Lucy.

Bromley went immediately to the station house to call the Cunningham's. He needed to talk to them about Suzy's boyfriend. Who was he? He was also waiting to hear back regarding Suzy's cell phone. Where her last call was made? It might well give him a clue as to where she was last night.

The police station was cold and gloomy. He turned on the lights and the heating. He would be there for some time. First he called the Cunningham's but they seemed shocked that Suzy would be meeting a boy in the middle of the night. They didn't know of any boyfriends. He asked about Suzy's cell phone. They said she had it on her when she left for the movies. Bromley knew her cell phone would be the best way of tracking her.

He had requested the tracking information and was ecstatic

to see Suzy had made a text message at twelve forty-nine to a number in Taipa. The number belonged to Staci Goodman. She had texted from the Hihi area.

Bromley felt he was getting closer and closer to finding her. Her boyfriend must live in Hihi somewhere. It was a small settlement. He picked up the phone and called his daughter, Lucy.

"Has Suzy ever mentioned a boy who lives in Hihi? He asked.

Lucy thought. "No," she replied.

Bromley called the cell phone of Staci and she answered immediately.

"Staci, here."

"Constable Bromley of the Mangonui Police," he announced. "Can you explain the text message you received from Suzy at twelve fifty-nine early this morning?

There was a long silence. "She just texted me to say not to pick her up and that she was getting a ride home," she replied.

"Who was giving her a ride home?" he asked patiently.

"She never said and I never asked," Suzy replied defiantly. "Is that all, officer? I have work to do."

"I will be in touch," said Bromley and hung up the phone.

It was going to be long night. Suzy was missing. It was now getting on to dusk. Almost twenty-four hours since she was last seen. It was time to get some help. He picked up the phone and called the media.

CHAPTER 27

The six o'clock news was a nightly event in New Zealand. Parents, pensioners and working folk huddled around the television to review the day's events. The local news always led the hour and tonight was no different. A picture of a pretty redheaded teenager filled the screen.

"Missing since last night," said the familiar news announcer. "Last seen at the Taipa Shopping center at eleven fifteen last night. Anyone seeing sixteen-year-old, Suzy Cunningham, in Taipa, Mangonui or the Hihi area or can offer information as to her whereabouts, please contact your local police station. She was wearing jeans, pink sweater, navy jacket, white Reeboks and carrying a blue backpack with a pink stripe."

Audrey almost dropped her wine glass. Hihi? Could that be the girl her tenant brought home last night? Her mind raced at the possibility. The police would be searching the area. She must find the girl first. Peering through the curtains she couldn't see any lights on in the cabin. *He must be sleeping,* she thought. *"I wonder where he took the girl?"*

Audrey paced up and down her little cottage. Her bedroom

and office sat at the far end facing the cabin. She always kept the curtains drawn. The other end of the cabin was divided by a row of chocolate brown curtains. A round table and chairs and the kitchen took up the other half of the cottage. Off the side of the kitchen there was a small laundry room that doubled as a spare single bedroom. It was here the fireplace stood providing the only heating for the small dwelling. Sliding doors opened up from the kitchen/dining area to the vast sea view. A patio and small steps lead up to a neatly mowed lawn area. Audrey could see her sheep grazing on the paddock over the wire fence. Their favorite spot was in front of the cottage looking out to sea. Periodically they would lift their heads and peer inside the cottage hoping to entice Audrey out with a bucket of multigrain nuts. Today Audrey was too preoccupied to respond to their woeful pleads.

She waited for a re-run of the night's headlines at six thirty. She jotted down the clothing the girl was wearing. There was no mention of the underwear and Audrey was definitely not going to contact the police to make enquiries. She was going to handle Mr. Gavin Jenkins herself.

Every few minutes she checked the cabin for any signs of life. Finally at eight thirty she saw the lights turn on. She was prepared with flashlight, headlight, raincoat, gumboots, and hat. She had already put the axe and wood splitter in the Rav4 along with a knife for protection. Audrey never owned a gun. She didn't really like to use physical violence but she may have no choice this time.

At nine fifteen she saw Gavin leave the cabin and head for the path along the ridge. He was dressed in raingear and was carrying black plastic bags. She noticed he was wearing a headlight like hers. She waited until he was out of sight and then followed him making sure she kept far enough behind him so he wouldn't hear her footsteps or the crackling of fallen branches on the track.

Halfway down the ridge he turned to the left and headed off into the dense bush. *What the hell?* Audrey thought. She followed him for a short distance terrified he would see the small beam of light she shone into the darkness. The rain had stopped but the cloudy, moonless night made it almost impossible to trek through the bush.

At first Audrey thought he might be looking for kiwi birds. After all it was a kiwi zone and the little native flightless birds were nocturnal, very illusive and difficult to spot. She would certainly feel stupid if that was all he was doing out here. But then she knew differently. He had stopped and was bending over struggling with something on the ground. He had hung a torch on a branch that shone brightly in the darkness.

Then she knew. It was the girl. He was putting her into black plastic rubbish bags. He flung her over his shoulder and headed in the opposite direction towards the gateway at the bottom of the driveway. She knew he would put the girl in his car and she would not have a chance to stop him. Quickly she retreated back to the ridge and back to the cottage where she grabbed a glass and large knife from the kitchen and ran out to his car parked in front of the cabin. She stabbed at the front tire with all her might. It was hard to penetrate the thick rubber, but perseverance prevailed. In case he had a spare tire she punctured one of the back tires too. A quick stomp on the glass sent glass fragments flying providing a viable reason for the resulting deflation. Quickly she returned to the cottage and peered out the bedroom window.

A few minutes later she saw him return to the cabin and then leave quickly and get into his car.

Audrey's heart was beating so fast. She hoped he wouldn't suspect her. He started driving towards the main driveway and then stopped. Audrey had turned out all her lights and was sitting in the darkness. She watched as he got out of the car and walked around the wheels. She saw panic set in. She had him. He could go nowhere. He would have to leave the girl in the bush and wait until tomorrow when he could get his tires fixed. Living in the country had its advantages. Getting a garage to come out at night was a long shot at best. And she was sure Gavin would not want to bring attention to himself or his car. She saw him return to the cabin and shut the glass sliding door with a bang. *Temper, Temper,* she thought. *I have you now.*

CHAPTER 28

Constable Bromley was deep in thought. He turned his mind back to last night. He had been to the Taipa Shopping Center during his surveillance. He hadn't seen anyone there. But he did recall seeing a couple of cars including a silver Toyota driving south on Highway ten towards Mangonui and possibly Hihi. He remembered thinking there was a young girl in the car with a male driver. He wished he had taken down the license plate number. It had looked like the same car he had spotted at the fish and chip shop in Mangonui. He decided to get in the patrol car and head off to Hihi and see if he could spot the car. It was a long shot. But sitting in the office was not easy to do when he had a countrywide search in place. He would forward his calls to the Kaitaia station in case anyone called with news from the broadcast. He knew they were already getting a team together and were scheduled to meet at his station late this evening. He just had time to make a quick search of the area and return in time to provide all the details to the team for their arrival.

It took only ten minutes to reach the small Hihi township. A painted circle on the town intersection created a legal round-about. He wondered how many residents actually drove around the painted parameter before turning right. He presumed only tourists would obey the sign. He drove down the three main roads and looked at each property for any sign of the silver Toyota. There were only a handful of residents living full time in the holiday village. Most homes were closed for the winter. He headed off towards the motor camp but still no sign of the car. He didn't really expect to find it but would have kicked himself if he hadn't at least tried. He made his way up the peninsula road towards his Uncle Bruce's property. He passed the motor camp but it looked deserted. He wouldn't be able to see any cars on the peninsula as the long driveways and bolted front gates restricted access. He turned around at Tiromoana just a few yards before Bruce's entranceway. He didn't have time for a family visit and headed back to the station.

He made a note to check any local owners of silver Toyota Celica. He wasn't sure of the year but it looked like it was a few years old. He might get lucky. He was sure it was the same car he had seen in Mangonui with the tall lean man driver. But he was at least in his fifties.

Suzy was meeting her boyfriend. The tall man was much too old to be her boyfriend. It must have been a coincidence he was in Taipa at the time the girl went missing. If he could locate the car and the man, he may have seen something. He made a quick call to the media with regards to the car. Maybe someone knew who the owner was. It was worth a chance.

CHAPTER 29

Bruce Bromley's adrenalin was pumping. He had heard on the ten thirty news the police were looking for a late model silver Toyota Celica. He remembered seeing a similar car at Audrey's the day before. He called Jimmy at the station.

"Jimmy, it's Bruce. I think I know where your silver Toyota Celica is. It is at Audrey's. I saw it parked outside the cabin. I am pretty sure it's the one you are looking for."

"Bloody Hell!" said Bromley. "I was just there. I turned around in her driveway. I took a quick trip around the area just a couple of hours ago. I am on my way. Thanks mate!"

He called to the group gathering in the main office. "Detective Burt we have a lead. It's the Toyota. Come with me."

They grabbed their coats and headed out into the cold blustery night.

Bruce was excited. Life was getting a lot more interesting since his new neighbor moved in next door. He decided to make his way down the grass track to Audrey's to see if the car was still there. Marge wanted to know where he was going so late. "Just checking the traps. I think I heard a couple kiwis on the big lawn." Marge didn't really care where he was going. He grabbed his spotlight and heavy coat, stepped into his gumboots and headed off across the grass.

The lights were out in the cottage. He did see the lights on in the cabin. The silver car was parked in the middle of the gravel round-a-bout. As he got closer he noticed two tires were flat. He knew he couldn't be spotted from behind the large concrete water tank and he made sure he had turned off his spotlight as he approached the property. It was difficult to see in the cloudy night, but he did confirm the car was indeed a Toyota Celica and was obviously a few years old. What's the chance this is the car Jimmy is looking for? He wondered.

It wasn't long before he heard a car coming up the driveway. He ducked back behind a row of large pine trees. He didn't want to be seen nosing around but he couldn't resist seeing what was to unfold.

The police car stopped outside the cabin. Constable Bromley and Detective Burt knocked on the cabin door. The door opened and the tall lean man Bromley had seen in Mangonui was standing in front of him. Bromley introduced himself and asked if it was his Toyota Celica parked in the driveway.

"Yes. It is my car," said the tall man. "Is there a problem?"

"Can we come in and have a word?" asked Bromley. "It will only take a few minutes of your time. We just have some questions as to your whereabouts last night between eleven p.m. and one a.m."

The tall man let them into the cheery little cabin and offered them a seat at the small square table. Bromley preferred to stand and waited for the tall man to reply.

"I was driving back from Kaitaia," he stated. "I arrived home here about twelve thirty."

"What were you doing in Kaitaia?" Bromley asked.

"Just checking out the area," he divulged begrudgingly.

"What is your full name?" Bromley asked.

"Gavin John Jenkins," he replied.

"You didn't pick up a young girl from Taipa did you?" Bromley asked, looking intently at the man.

"No. I was alone" he replied quietly. "I don't know anyone in the area. Only been here a few days."

"Did you see a young girl at the Taipa shopping center when you passed?" he asked.

"Can't say I did." said the man. It was raining heavily on my trip home and I had a full time job just watching the road."

Bromley looked around the cabin. Everything was clean and orderly. Not a sign of any female. Just rain gear and boots. Bromley noticed the bottom of the raincoat was covered in fresh mud.

"Have you been out this evening?" he asked.

"Just went outside to look for kiwis a couple of hours ago," he said.

"Find any?" Bromley asked.

"Nope. Not a one," he replied. "Is there anything else I can help you with?"

"We would like to look over your car if it is not a problem" Bromley said.

"Do you have a warrant?" the man asked.

"I can soon get one" Bromley said abruptly.

"Great" said the man. "When you get the warrant you can search the car," he said walking towards the door and showing the policemen politely through. "Goodnight officers."

"We will be back with a warrant," said Bromley as they left.

On the drive back to the station they agreed Gavin Jenkins was a shifty sort of guy and obviously had something to hide in his car. Maybe it was just an unregistered firearm or drugs. They would be back in the morning with a warrant. Unfortunately, it would give Mr. Jenkins plenty of time to get rid of anything untoward.

Both men had no idea they were watched intently by two sets of peering eyes from dark places.

As they pulled out of the driveway onto the peninsula road Bromley called the station and ordered a patrol car and a couple of detectives to do an all-night surveillance of the Hihi area. Just in case Mr. Jenkins decided to do a scarper. He also arranged a warrant to search the whole wooded area surrounding the property first thing in the morning.

CHAPTER 30

Audrey couldn't believe her eyes when she saw the police car park outside the cabin and two policemen go inside. She quickly sneaked out of the cottage and around the back of the cabin. The bathroom window was slightly ajar and she could hear voices inside. They were asking Gavin about his car and where he had been last night. She heard Gavin refuse to let them search his car and she knew the policemen would be back with a warrant. How did they know about the car? Was he seen driving in the area? He must have been. But how did they know where he lived? So many questions left unanswered.

Audrey had heard about the car and the description of the tall lean man on the late-night news and knew she had to work quickly to deal with Mr. Jenkins before the police got their hands on him. She must be ready to act at any moment. That would mean keeping awake most of the night. He had to go to sleep sometime.

She wondered what was in his car he didn't want the police to find. She hoped it was a gun. A gun would certainly come in handy. Audrey heard a noise coming from the top paddock. She walked over towards the sound and shone her torch. She thought she saw a movement in the forest and stood still and waited. Nothing. It must have been her imagination. She returned to the cottage and kept the lights low while she waited and watched.

Gavin left the cabin and headed towards his car and returned a moment later carrying a bag. Immediately he was back in the car, and she waited for what seemed an eternity. *He must be getting rid of any evidence,* she thought. Her suspicions were correct. She could see the inside light in the car and it was obvious he was wiping the whole interior. She knew it made no difference if he wiped all evidence of the girl. She had the best evidence tucked away safely in the cottage.

Soon the cops would be back and would have a warrant to search not only the car - but also the whole property. She had been through that before and knew they would have dogs that could find the girl in no time. She must work quickly and now she knew exactly what she must do.

CHAPTER 31

Gavin was in fast mode. First he had to get rid of any evidence that might be in his car. Then he must move the girl to a safer place - off the property - but how? That was the question. He had no drivable vehicle. There was always Audrey's Rav4 but he knew she would suspect him wanting to borrow it this late at night. He would have to go too far to steal a car and the cops could be watching the area. After cleaning the car and wiping every trace of the girl away, he returned to the cabin to develop a plan of attack.

Pacing up and down he realized he was screwed. He opened the bag and took out his 22- rifle. He loaded it and placed it on the bed beside him. He still had the handcuffs and duct tape he was planning of disposing with the girl. Now it was too late. She was about twenty meters from the front gate down a steep bank and hidden by dense bush. It would only take a police dog minutes to find her. He had not even covered her knowing he was going to put her in his car and take her to the place he had found only this morning. That seemed liked days ago. He looked at the time. It was just after midnight. He only had about seven hours until daylight. He put his head in his hands and felt despair like never before. Then he saw her. Standing at the glass door staring straight at him.

Her first words when he opened the door were "You have no choice. We must move the body. The roads are not safe. I have a better plan. Hurry, we don't have much time."

"Why? Why would you want to help me?" He was stunned. How did she know?

"Never mind that," she said. "Follow me."

She went to the small shed attached to the cottage and opened the old wooden doors and pulled out a red dolly.

"Go get the girl and put her in my car and drive her back here," she said, handing him a large clear plastic bag. "Make sure she is completely encased in the bag before you put her in the back of my car and put her backpack in the bag with her. We don't want any DNA getting into my car or on our clothes. Hurry. The keys are in the car."

Gavin was still trying to make sense of the situation. He followed her instructions without question. He retrieved the handcuffs and tape, leaving the gun in the cabin. As he reached the gate at the far end of the drive he was careful to check if anyone was lurking about.

It was quiet. He climbed down into the bank to retrieve the girl and the backpack. The road was silent. He put them both into the plastic bag along with the handcuffs and tape and tied the end with a piece of string he had found in the car. With difficulty he climbed up the slippery bank, opened the back door of the Rav4 and lifted the body inside. When he returned to the parking area, he saw Audrey standing there with the dolly and a couple of pairs of headlights.

"Put her on the dolly," she said, "and we will take her down pinecone track to the front beach. I have a tinny boat there and we can take her out into the bay and dump her."

It wasn't easy on the slippery track. Recent rain had made the path treacherous and the girl kept falling off the dolly. It was easier to lay the dolly almost flat and push it downhill over tree roots and rugged terrain. It took a good five minutes to reach the bottom of the ridge and then there were hundred steps down to the beach. They took the girl off the dolly, tied a long rope to the bag and lowered her over the cliff onto the rocky beach below.

Audrey kept her little tin boat tied to a huge pohutukawa tree. She untied the boat and grabbed the oars. They put the body bag into the boat and pushed the tin boat over the stony beach into the waves. Audrey's beach could not be seen from the Hihi Township. They thought the bay might be under surveillance, so they headed away from Hihi beach and out into the open sea. Karikari peninsula, directly across the bay provided relative shelter and the waves, although choppy were manageable. Gavin did the rowing while Audrey undid the rope from the plastic body bag. Together they released the contents from the bag and watched as the girl slipped into the cold swell of the Pacific Ocean.

They rowed back in silence. The noise of the waves and the wind prevented them from having any audible conversation. The deed was done. The girl would not be found.

Gavin helped Audrey secure the boat on the beach and together they made their way back up the muddy steps to the top of the ridge. Gavin dragged the dolly back up to the shed where they washed it clean. Audrey put it neatly back in its place behind the weedwhacker and garden tools.

"Are you going to explain why you are helping me?" asked Gavin.

"I knew it was you," she said. "I followed you and saw you move the girl."

"Was it you who called the police" he asked.

"Hell no!" she said with surprise. "Why would I do that? I don't want any trouble here. Do you have anything else that needs to be disposed of before the police arrive with their warrant?"

Gavin thought about the loaded gun still in the cabin. He wondered if he should tell her about it. "I have a rifle," he confessed.

"Has it been fired?" she asked. "Did you use it on the girl? Is it registered to you?"

"No it hasn't been fired. I didn't kill the girl with it and, yes, it is registered in my name."

"Then best to leave it in the cabin. You can always say that was the reason you didn't want them to search your car. You thought it might create a problem. Anything else?" She asked. "Have you cleaned away all traces of the girl in the cabin?"

"Yes," he replied suddenly feeling completely exhausted.

"Good. Then let's get some sleep. We can talk in the morning." Audrey turned and walked towards the cottage.

Gavin returned to the cabin and closed the door. He pulled the curtains, removed his jacket and boots, unloaded the gun and placed the gun and the bullets into the tin box and locked it away in the dresser. The police would find it tomorrow. It can do him no harm. He fell on the bed and still fully clothed, fell asleep.

CHAPTER 32

A udrey looked at the bedside clock as she got into bed. It was two thirty, leaving only a few hours before the police would arrive with their search warrant. She knew she wanted no trouble with the police. The well-publicized murders only a year ago in her hometown of Kaeo would only stir up questions. Body parts had been found on her property there. They had found the culprit and he was now locked away in the local jail. But, coincidences, when it comes to murder, are red flags to the police. She presumed the local police would be working with the Kaitaia police and the Kaeo police would not be involved.

Best to remove herself from the scene. She would leave early in the morning for Kaitaia. Do some shopping at the Warehouse. Maybe stop by the demolition yard and see if they have anything she can use for her continuous renovations. She leaned over and set the alarm for seven a.m.

Car tires on the gravel driveway awakened her. "Damn" she said. "They are earlier than I would have thought." She leaped out of bed and put the missing girl's panties, still wrapped in the paper towel, at the bottom of her underwear drawer just in case they had a warrant to search her cottage too.

She presumed Gavin would also be asleep as she heard them knocking at his door. There were cars everywhere and dogs. There was no doubt they suspected Gavin of the girl's disappearance. She only hoped they had eliminated any evidence, leaving them with nothing but their injured pride to take back to the station.

She couldn't leave anyway. The cars had blocked her in. Gavin's car was still in the turnaround area with flat tires. She realized her fingerprints were on the broken glass and decided to remove the pieces. After all they were a hazard to any car.

She quickly dressed, grabbed a bucket and headed off across the lawn to the driveway.

"Morning," a police officer said. "I am Detective Burt. Sorry to disturb you but we have a warrant to search the cabin, the Toyota and the premises."

"What for?" she asked.

"We believe your tenant, Mr. Jenkins may be a person of interest in the disappearance of the Cunningham girl," he said. "Do you have time to answer some questions?"

"Yes, of course" she responded with a friendly smile. She knew picking up the broken glass would be too suspicious now and invited the policeman into the cottage.

"Would you like a cup of tea?" she asked.

"That would be nice," he said taking off his hat and placing it on the table.

Audrey put on the jug and invited him to sit at the table.

"Nice property you have here," he said. "How long have you lived here?"

"Oh I have been fixing it up for the past six months or so but just moved in a few days ago," she replied.

"When did Mr. Jenkins move into the cabin?" he asked.

"Actually, about the same time as I moved in" she responded. "Nice man, very quiet and polite. Said he came here for the fishing. We have a great fishing spot here off table rock."

Audrey stood to make the tea and plated some chocolate biscuits. As she returned to the table she asked, "Why do you suspect Gavin? I can't imagine he would be involved in anyway. He has hardly left the cabin since he arrived."

"His car was seen close to where the girl went missing," he said. And he wouldn't let us search his car last night which naturally lays suspicion on him."

"He seems like a private person," she said. "Maybe he just doesn't like people touching his things."

"How well do you know Mr. Jenkins?" he asked.

"Oh, I don't know him. He applied to the ad I put on 'Trade Me. He is on a six month's lease" she replied.

The policeman finished his tea and stood up to leave. "Better get back to it," he said. "Thanks for the tea."

"Glad to help," said Audrey. "Let me know if there is anything else you need.

CHAPTER 33

Constable Bromley was prepared for a dawn raid. It was six forty-five when they arrived at Audrey's property. The full team was there, forensics, detectives and police dogs. Bromley had a gut feeling Jenkins was involved. All he had to do was find some evidence that tied him to the missing girl.

One team started on the Toyota, another team on the cabin and a third team with the dogs started searching the fourteen-acre bush property. It was a big job. By noon they had found nothing.

Fingerprints had been taken from the car and the cabin and it would take time to run them through the system. They took Jenkins' fingerprints for reference. The dogs had made a couple of stops in the bush but no sign of the girl or her belongings could be found. By two in the afternoon the teams packed up and left the property empty handed. Bromley was frustrated.

A couple of things played on his mind. Why was Jenkins' car in the middle of the driveway with two punctured tires? Why had Jenkins refused the let them search the car the night before?

They had found a .22 caliber rifle. He kept it in a locked large tin box. Upon request Jenkins had opened the box and the police checked the weapon. It had not been fired recently and Jenkins had paperwork showing it was fully licensed.

Detective Burt had questioned Audrey in the cottage. "Nice lady," he said. "She doesn't think Jenkins would be involved in the disappearance of the girl. Said he just likes to go fishing and keep to himself. Looks as though we are wrong about the guy. He never left the property last night we had it watched from the time we left last night to the time we arrived this morning. His car has a couple of flats anyway."

"We need to find her boyfriend," said Constable Bromley. "I think that girl Staci knows more about this than she has told us. I am going to track that girl down and bring her into the station."

Detective Burt had formed his own opinion about Jenkins. He seemed like a quiet mannered man who valued his privacy. A murderer or rapist didn't seem to fit his profile. Burt thought Bromley was on the wrong track.

"Yes. I agree. Let's check out the Staci girl. There is more to this than meets the eye. I will run a background check on the girl. See if I come up with anything."

When they arrived back at the station they were inundated with messages from the public who had information about the car, the tall lean man and the girl herself. It was going to be long day sifting through all the information and determining if any of it had any relevance to the case.

CHAPTER 34

Staci was feeling particularly nervous this morning. She had seen the news last night and again this morning and knew the cops were still searching for Suzy. If they didn't find her soon she was in deep shit. She was responsible for Suzy and Lucy working the streets that night. They had tracked the text message to her and they would want to talk to her again. She had been taking a cut from Suzy's jobs and it had been working out great. She wasn't pleased when Suzy said Lucy wanted to work that night also. Now Lucy was a threat. If she talked she would be back in court again. She already had a record on file with the police of prostituting young girls under the legal age. This time it would mean a jail sentence.

Her cell phone rang and as expected, it was Constable Bromley. She cursed that she hadn't thrown away the phone but this was the number she generated work from and she needed the work.

"Staci," she answered.

"Constable Bromley here. We need you to come to the

Mangonui Police Station. We have a few questions. When can you make it in?"

"I am in Whangarei," replied Staci. "It will take me a couple of hours to get there. Can't you ask me the questions over the phone?"

"When are you returning home?' he asked

"I am home. I have moved to Whangarei. Been here since yesterday."

"Any reason you have moved?" Bromley asked.

"Just needed a change," said Staci.

"I will arrange to have you picked up. What is your address?"

Staci told him her address and agreed to be ready at eight a.m. for the trip to Mangonui.

"Shit! Bloody shit!" swore Staci. Where the hell is Suzy? Why hasn't she called me? She decided to call Suzy's home number and talk to her parent to enquire if they have heard anything and to say she was worried.

Suzy's father answered the phone. Staci had met him at the summer camp but doubted if he remembered. She guessed the police had already told them she had dropped off Suzy at the Taipa Shops. She asked if they had heard from Suzy yet. He sounded so distraught.

"No, we have not heard from her and have no idea where she is," he said. "Why did you leave her alone in the dark at the deserted shopping center?" he accused Staci.

"I am so sorry. She said she had arranged to meet someone there and they were driving her home" she said apologetically. "I thought she had told you." She paused. "Have you spoken to her friend, Lucy?" asked Staci.

Suzy's father said, "Lucy doesn't know where she is either. After all her father is heading the case. If she knew anything she would have told him."

"Her father?" asked Staci.

"Constable Bromley. Lucy's father" Mark Cunningham said.

"Oh. Of course," said Staci in complete shock. "I am so sorry Mr. Cunningham. I must go. Bye."

Staci sat down at her computer and did a search on Constable Bromley. Sure enough he was the guy in charge of the case. The case of the missing girl from Mangonui was all over the web. There was a photo of the policeman and his family at a local charity event. She recognized Lucy immediately.

Now she was in double deep shit. Lucy was sure to talk before long. She wasn't looking forward to her visit to the police station tomorrow. Should she just come clean? It was going to get out anyway soon. At least they might find Suzy or the john who picked her up for a full night of teenage sex. What would Constable Bromley think when he found out his daughter was doing tricks too. The media would go crazy.

CHAPTER 35

Gavin couldn't believe his luck. Saved by the buxom blonde landlady. Who would have thought? He made his way over to the cottage to thank her. Why she would help him he had no idea. There was definitely more to Audrey than meets the eye. He found her resting on a lounge chair on the front lawn overlooking the ocean. The storm had vanished leaving blue skies, puffy white clouds and sparking turquoise water creating a view of sheer wonder. As he approached her he noticed a bottle of Lindauer Brut Cuvee and two glasses sitting on the side table.

"What's the occasion?" he asked cheekily.

"Please join me" she replied grinning from ear to ear. "It's time to celebrate."

"Cheers!" Gavin toasted as they clicked glasses and watched a fishing boat chugging out to sea.

There was no need for words. They sat in silence both deep in thought as they allowed the champagne to lift their senses and wipe away the memory of the previous night.

"I am guessing they didn't find anything?" she asked Gavin.

"Nope. Not a thing. They checked my rifle to see if it had been fired and took my fingerprints."

"No previous record?" she asked.

"No, clean as a whistle," he smiled as he stretched his long legs and leaned back on the lounger.

"Why did you pick up the girl?" she asked.

"She was a street worker. I was just looking for a bit of fun," he replied easily.

Gavin didn't notice the change in Audrey's eyes. Her emotions were well hidden by her huge sunglasses she always wore.

He is no different from any other man, she thought. And in time he would have to pay for what he had done. But in the meantime, he was a pleasant distraction from her newly found poverty and self-incriminations.

Audrey had a roast of pork in the oven. She liked to eat early. She asked Gavin if he wanted to join her for dinner. He gratefully accepted having not had a good meal for the last couple of days.

They sat outside drinking until the sun fell from the sky and the early evening air cooled.

Audrey turned on iTunes and played a selection of her favorite blues. They opened their third bottle and danced in joint inebriated abandonment. It felt good to have some fun. A strange couple they made. The tall lean man and the short, big breasted blonde. They were uncomfortable strangers in life but cooperating allies in crime.

By the time they had finished Audrey's roast dinner, complete with gravy and homemade applesauce, both were feeling the strain of the sleepless night. They said goodnight and retreated to their respective beds for the first good night's sleep in days.

CHAPTER 36

It was another early start at the Mangonui Police Station. The team was already assembled, and Constable Bromley had just finished preparing the interrogation room for Staci's arrival. At seven thirty the first team left for the local high school to interview Suzy's school friends hoping to locate the boyfriend of interest.

The Kaitaia team with dog handlers were searching the area around the Taipa Shopping Center for any clues. Detective Burt and Constable Bromley were returning leads from the overwhelming media response.

They had sorted the leads into three categories: car, man, and Suzy. Having located the car and the man, they now concentrated on any leads with a reference to Suzy. One lead in particular caught Detective Burt's interest. The message read:

Client of Suzy
Wants to stay anonymous
Has information of interest
Phone....

"What the hell? A client? What sort of client? Bromley picked up the phone and made the call.

"Yep," a man's deep voice answered.

"Constable Bromley here. You have some information regarding the missing girl, Suzy Cunningham?"

"Don't want to give my name. But I can tell you that Suzy was no angel. I picked her up from the Taipa shopping center twice in the past month. She is a street bunny if you know what I mean. Shame she is missing. I wanted to let you know in case you didn't know she was a sex worker."

"Are you sure you are talking about the same girl?" Bromley asked in shock.

"Absolutely. I saw her photo on the news. That's Suzy all right. She works under the name of Red. Charges $100 bucks an hour. Worth every dollar."

"Did you know she was only sixteen years old?" asked Bromley.

"Didn't know until I heard it on the news," said the man. "She sure doesn't look it. Thought she was at least eighteen. She wears leather boots, mini skirt and a face full of makeup. That's all I've got to say. Hope you find her mate."

Constable Bromley sat dazed in his chair. Suzy is Lucy's best friend. She must know Suzy was working the streets. His heart sunk as he thought of his innocent little daughter and hoped she wasn't involved in any way.

This changed things. There was no boyfriend. A john had obviously picked her up. Bromley wished the Taipa Shopping center had a security camera. It didn't. Beta Electrical and the other shops had security systems in store. But there was nothing covering the car park area. He tried to recall the night. The traffic had been almost non-existent. He had seen a couple of cars that night, but the silver Toyota was the only car he remembered on the road during the time in question. Maybe Jenkins had picked up the girl and returned her an hour later. But he couldn't prove anything. This case was getting more and more complicated. How was he going to tell Suzy's parents? They were already suffering. Hearing their sweet daughter was a working girl would only put them into total despair.

Bromley radioed the teams with the update. Focus was now concentrated on Suzy's after school activities. He decided to wait to talk to Suzy's parents until he could confirm the new information.

As the morning progressed Bromley and Burt continued to return calls. Another john who wouldn't give his name confirmed Suzy was indeed "Red," a regular sex worker. At ten-thirty Staci entered the police station accompanied by a detective from the Whangarei station. Bromley showed Stacy into the interrogation room and closed the door behind them.

CHAPTER 37

Bruce Bromley was enjoying his morning cup of tea seated at the wooden bench on the outside deck and gazing out at the bright sun glistening on the cool blue sea. The winterless far north, as it was commonly referred to, was living up to its reputation. It was a perfect day to take the boat out and do some fishing. He considered asking Audrey to accompany him but with all that had been going on over there, he knew today was not the day to get involved. Instead, he decided to call a couple of mates who lived further up the peninsula. They were avid fishermen and always up for a trip out to sea.

By late morning his mates had arrived with their fishing gear in tow and they made their way down to his private beach. Bruce's hundred acres included three private beaches, wide-open grassland and at least eighty acres of native bush. His expansive modern home sat perched on the edge of a ridge overlooking the ocean.

Bruce kept his boat in one of the large sheds on the property. They towed the boat with the tractor down to the water's edge. Bruce loved this beach. It was the only sandy beach on the rocky peninsula. Today they had planned to take the boat out to sea past the Kerikeri peninsula in the hope of catching some yellow fish tuna.

They had already loaded three-dozen beers into the boat and all the fishing gear. Bruce launched the boat into the water and returned the tractor to the beach. With all onboard they headed out towards the open sea.

Bruce's friends loved to gossip. Today was no exception. They had their own opinions as to where the red headed girl was.

"Most probably shacked up with her boyfriend," one said.

"She's a pretty girl," said the other.

Bruce couldn't resist himself. "Ya know they did a search of my neighbor's property yesterday," he said. "I called them to let them know a silver Toyota Celica was parked there, like the one they were looking for. They were there most of the day. I guess they didn't find anything, or we would have heard something. My nephew is leading the case. He's a smart guy."

Five minutes out into the bay they saw something bobbing in the water.

"Hey" one of the guys called out "looks like something in the water."

Bruce headed off in the direction of the object. As they got closer they saw it was a blue backpack. "It has a pink stripe like they showed on the news," he shouted over the engine. "Grab a pole and we will fish it in." With the bag on board the guys looked inside to see if they could identify the owner. It was full of clothes, jeans, jacket, reebok shoes.

"Shit! It is the girl's bag alright," Bruce said. "We had better head back to shore and get it to the police. Bloody hell. There goes our fishing."

The guys agreed and they turned the boat around and headed for shore. Bruce called his nephew from his cell phone but was told he was out of the station. He left a message saying they had found the bag and was bringing it into the station. He tried his nephew's cell phone but there was no answer. He left the same message.

"Looks bad," he said to the guys. "If her bag is floating in the ocean, she could be there too!"

There was a somber mood as they docked and towed the boat to the shed. The guys offered to wash the boat so Bruce could head off into Mangonui with the bag.

CHAPTER 38

Staci was finally released from the station. They even offered to drive her back to Whangarei as the local detective was heading back anyway. It had been really awful and she was feeling quite sick over the whole thing.

They say confession is good for the soul. She didn't think her soul felt any better than her stomach. Having to say that she had dropped Suzy off at the shopping center so she could work was bad enough but Constable Bromley wanted to know about his daughter and if she was involved in the prostitution business too. That was the hardest part. She had considered lying and saying she only dropped Suzy there and had taken Lucy home straight away but Constable Bromley's stuck-up attitude really pissed Staci off. He was acting holier than thou and judging her for being a working girl as though she was worthless, just a tramp.

Staci got really mad and told him, right to his face, "Who are you to judge me? Your daughter does tricks too, you know. She was also working that night. That's right! You ask her! You ask her what time she got home. It was after one in the morning when I dropped her off."

She saw the policeman's face turn ashen. Shocked. He slumped forward as if all the wind had just been punched out of him. Staci knew things would never be the same for him. *It served him right,* she thought as she was driven home. He made me do it. After all, it is the truth. I didn't make Suzy or Lucy work that night. They asked me for the ride there. No more. I have a good job at the Brothel in Whangarei with good money.

She considered herself lucky. The police didn't know she got a cut from Suzy's jobs. She had told Constable Bromley she had just dropped them off and picked them up at their request. Nothing illegal in that. She was glad she was out of the street business. Before long she will have saved enough to start her own brothel. She only needed another twenty thousand dollars. It was a shame no one other than her and Detective Bromley were in the in the room during the interrogation. It might have been good to have some witnesses.

CHAPTER 39

Constable Bromley wasn't answering his cell phone. He saw it was his uncle calling but he just couldn't face talking to anyone right now. He had left the station after interviewing Staci. The news his daughter was doing tricks on the street was just too much to bear. He couldn't tell his wife. He didn't even have the guts to confront his daughter. He just didn't want to know. These things happened to other people. His reputation in the police force would be ruined. His daughter was only sixteen. What was she thinking? Legalized prostitution in New Zealand was bad enough but young teenagers were idolizing the working girls.

Too many American television programs portraying porn queens as role models, he thought. Even today's teen pop stars are twerking and singing almost naked.

Young girls thought they could become rich by having sex. "Why work for minimum wage when you can earn a hundred bucks an hour," he would hear teens say as they were picked up off the streets. Johns didn't help. They often preferred the younger girls and as long as there was a market, young girls would oblige.

He had read naked selfies were a growing phenomenon amongst teens and hoped his daughter was not participating in this trend. Now that seemed immaterial compared to selling her body for money.

A good thirty minutes had gone by and he was still sitting in his car watching the pleasure boats coming and going in the bay. He knew he must make a move. He looked at his phone, it was two o'clock. Lucy wouldn't be home until after four. He decided to head back to the station but first he returned the call to his uncle.

CHAPTER 40

Ll was breaking loose at the Mangonui Police Station. News had travelled fast across the region. Police from neighboring stations were called in to assist as soon as the news of the girl's backpack having been found in Hihi bay was released. A search team was scouring the bay looking for any signs of the missing girl.

Constable Bromley was preoccupied with the thought of his own daughter being involved somehow. He knew once the media got hold of the latest information his whole career was in jeopardy. He must talk to his daughter, but first he should talk to Mary. He knew his daughter was involved somehow and he should take himself off the case.

He just hoped they didn't find the girl dead in the bay. Maybe she was still alive somewhere. He would wait until the bay was searched before making a decision. If he were lucky, the case would be solved without anyone knowing about Lucy. But he didn't like his chances. The girl had been missing for almost seventy-two hours and as time progresses the chances of finding the girl become more and more difficult.

He decided to head off to Hihi Bay and see how the search was progressing. Interviewing his daughter could wait.

The bay was buzzing with activity. Locals were congregating around the shoreline. Police cars lined the street from the little one-way bridge to the motor camp. Only residents were allowed through the area. Bromley noticed a couple sitting in a blue Rav4. It was Audrey and Jenkins. As soon as he spotted them he saw them drive off up Peninsula Road.

"Bloody hell," he muttered under his breath. "Come to the scene of the crime – eh?"

He was sure Jenkins had something to do with the missing girl and he would find out just what that was.

CHAPTER 41

Audrey knew she must act soon. Gavin Jenkins was becoming a liability. The local cop had seen them at the beach. Curiosity had led them down to the beach. By late afternoon the bay was bobbing with police launches. Audrey wondered what they were doing or, worse still, what they had found.

"It's the missing girl. They found her backpack floating in the bay. They are searching for the girl" wide-eyed women affronted Audrey in obvious shock.

Audrey and Gavin were horrified. The bag must have floated to the surface. The girl's body could either be washed out to sea or washed up on shore. They hoped the first scenario was true. Gavin would be in deep shit if the body was found. He knew they would have his DNA if it weren't completely diluted by seawater.

At dusk the local garage finally arrived to fix Gavin's car tires. Audrey and Gavin watched the police carrying out their search from the front lawn until it became too dark and the launches returned to shore.

Audrey knew tonight she must make Gavin pay for what he had done. If she waited any longer he might be arrested and she would miss the opportunity. She would wait until dark then make her move. First she would make her favorite concoction of champagne and GHB powder. Just enough to send him to sleep and then she could set the scene.

Audrey liked to use GHB. She had been successful before with this drug. It took away any personal violence from her projects and always achieved excellent results. Tonight it would be more messy - but necessary.

She had arranged with Gavin to meet in his cabin for a nightcap at nine o'clock. She felt a rush of excitement. All she needed was a nice hot bath. She would wash her hair, put on makeup and wear her sexiest black top with her new skinny jeans. The only skinny part of Audrey was from the hips down and she liked to emphasize this feature.

By nine o'clock she was dressed and ready for a night of sheer joy. "I look fantastic" she chuckled as she poured her third glass of champagne. She took the new bottle over to Gavin's and knocked on the door.

CHAPTER 42

Lucy sat at the dinner table dreading what was about to happen. Her Dad wouldn't look at her in the eye. Her Mother seemed to be in shock. They knew. She just knew that they knew. They sat in silence eating pork curry and rice. It was her favorite and she felt guilty her mother had made it and now she had ruined everything.

Finally, her father spoke. "Your Mother and I have been talking" he began. "I found out something today that I needed to discuss with her, and now we need to discuss it with you."

Here it comes, she thought. "What is it?" she asked as innocently as she could.

"Staci came into the station today" he said.

"Why?" Lucy asked as she felt her face redden and pulse race.

"I brought her in to be interviewed. She told me Suzy was a prostitute, a sex worker. She said she had been doing it for some time now. Did you know she was doing that?" He asked.

Lucy didn't answer. She didn't know what her father knew and she didn't want to incriminate herself.

"Lucy? Did you know?" Her Father asked again more

urgently. "Did you know she was working the streets for God's sake?"

Lucy knew her Father was furious. "Yes, I knew." She shouted as she pushed back her chair and started to leave the room.

"Come back here. I haven't finished!" he shouted.

Lucy stopped in her tracks and turned towards him. "I don't want to talk about it," she said.

"Well, you have no choice. Either you talk about it here or you will talk about it in the station. And there it won't just be you and me. It will be on the record. So if you have something to say, you had better say it now," he demanded.

Lucy sat back down at the table. "OK, what do you want to know?"

"How long has Suzy been working the streets?" he asked.

"Since she went to summer camp. She met Staci there and now she works regularly.

Her parents don't know. They think she is out with friends."

"That night did you see who picked her up?"

"No," Lucy replied. She knew what was coming next.

"Why not?" he asked.

"Because when Staci and I dropped of Suzy at the shops Staci took me straight home," she replied.

"Do you know who might have picked her up?" he prodded further.

"No. I have no idea. She didn't talk about her johns," said Lucy. "And I didn't want to know about them."

"Have you ever worked with Suzy or Staci?" he asked the dreaded question.

Lucy looked at him straight in the eyes and said "Of course not. Why would you ask such a thing?" She could see relief soften his face. She knew she had done the right thing. After all, it was only once, and they would never know.

Constable Bromley watched as his daughter left the table. She seemed so little and innocent. How did all this happen? He wondered.

Tomorrow they would continue to search the bay. It would be an early start, which meant an early night. He might even drive up to Audrey's and have another talk with Gavin Jenkins. He was sure he saw a girl in his car that night. Maybe he was the john. He decided to call his uncle.

"Bruce, it's Jimmy. No, Nothing yet. I still think that guy, Jenkins, is mixed up in this somehow. Thanks for all your help today. Talk to you tomorrow." He hung up and went to bed.

CHAPTER 43

Bruce couldn't settle down. Finding the girls bag in the bay made it more personal somehow. Jimmy still believed Jenkins was involved. He decided to take a walk in the moonlit night. Maybe he could see what was going on next door. He made his usual excuse about checking the traps, donned his gumboots, grabbed his jacket and headed off into the night.

It was quite a walk between the two properties. He figured it was about three hundred yards between his house and the cottage. The grassed path only went up to the boundary line. From there he made his way through the thick bush where he could clearly see both the cottage and the cabin.

The lights were on in both buildings. He sat down on an old tree stump and lit up a ciggy. Marge wouldn't let him smoke in the house. Not like the old days. Nothing was like the old days.

He was feeling quite the detective. He could see Jenkins' silhouette walking around in the cabin. He had the curtains pulled but they didn't block out the light. He looked at his watch it was almost nine. He shouldn't be too late or Marge would worry. He would give it another ten minutes and then he should head on back.

He saw her. She was all dolled up and carrying a bottle of wine. She knocked at the cabin door. Jenkins appeared looking dressed for a night on the town. "Bloody hell" he muttered. "She has the hots for Jenkins!" Bruce suddenly felt deflated. He had hoped he might have a chance with Audrey. He stubbed out his ciggy on the wet ground and made his way back home to Marge.

It wasn't until he and Marge were tucked up in bed that he heard the shot. They had just turned off the nightly news. He looked at the clock, it was eleven. He wondered who was out pig hunting. It wasn't unusual to hear shots at night. The yearly pig hunting competition was taking place over the next couple of days and the locals were out trying to win first prize for the biggest pig. He wasn't participating this year. But he might go to the final night booze up to see who had won. Funny, the shot seemed to come from over Audrey's way. Must be further down the valley. He couldn't imagine Audrey and Jenkins out shooting pigs, they weren't really dressed for hunting. He turned out the light, rolled over and placed his back next to Marge. She was like a heater in bed. Good ol' Marge. She wasn't so bad after all.

CHAPTER 44

Audrey remembered the time when she was at a life planning retreat in Santa Barbara. One day the group congregated on the sandy beach opposite the hotel. One member of the group was instructed to attempt to get from point A to point B: an approximate distance of fifty meters. The rest of the group was instructed to prevent the member from achieving that task. They were to try and trip them up, hold them, and stop them in any way they could without using actual physical violence. Each individual member of the group fought their way through the group reaching their goal with sheer joy and a positive sense of self-achievement.

When Audrey broke through the human roadblocks and made it to the finishing line, she collapsed in utter despair. Life had been hard for her. The physical task of reliving the hardship was too much to bear. She discovered that achieving the goal did not compensate for the unbearable pain of taking life's journey. She understood then she was different.

It was midnight and she had finished another project. She had once again reached her goal. Over the past few years she had developed a coping system that worked for her. The fear and loathing that had consumed her everyday life was now replaced with a reckoning. All the men who had derided her during her childhood, youth and adulthood were responsible now for her actions.

She felt no guilt and no remorse and, more importantly, she now felt what others felt; a sense of self achievement when carrying out a task and completing it. Careful planning and execution has resulted in success once again.

Audrey knew her actions were socially and legally unacceptable. The next few days were critical. She enjoyed the knowledge that she was never suspected in her crimes. Her pleasant demeanor created a successful mask of deceit and she was proficient in leading the police in any direction she chose.

First thing tomorrow she would put her plan into action. Tonight she would enjoy a well-deserved sleep.

CHAPTER 45

It was six o'clock when the alarm woke Constable Bromley. He turned to look at Mary who was still sleeping. She looked like an angel. Her long, dark, wavy hair spread across the pillow. He loved her hair. She was a beautiful woman. His daughters, thank goodness, took after her. His thoughts went to Lucy, their first child. He remembered she was born with dark hair and by the age of two it reached her shoulders. He hoped Lucy had told him the truth last night. That she had never prostituted herself. He would never forgive himself if she had. It was his responsibility as a father and parent to engrain good morals into her everyday life and he hoped he had achieved that. He felt guilty his job took him away from home so often. He must try to spend more time with the kids. Maybe he could take some time off when this case was solved.

He swung his legs over the side of the bed and rested his hands in his head. It was going to be a long day - an important day. Today they would find the girl. He just knew it. They had planned to begin the search at daybreak. Which meant he must get down to the beach. He grabbed a coffee and a banana muffin and made his way over to the station next door.

The station was alive with activity. The search teams had already left for Doubtless Bay. One team headed for Hihi beach and the other team for Mangonui Harbor. Divers would search the coastline and the bay for any sign of the girl. It was a huge task as the bay had over seventy kilometers of coastline. The Doubtless Bay area extended from Taupo Bay in the east to the Karikari Peninsula in the west. It included the settlements of Hihi, Coopers Beach, Cable Bay, Taipa and Whatuwhiwhi, with its center in busy Mangonui.

Bromley had also sent a team to search three more isolated beaches in case the girl's body had washed ashore there. The coastguard was searching the coastline in the more remote areas of the bay.

Upon arrival at Hihi Beach he was inundated with media. They wanted to know what they expected to find. Bromley had little information to give them.

"The case is still in progress," he reported. "We have search teams in the bay and surrounding coastline. We have nothing new to report to date but we will keep you informed as the day progresses."

Bromley was uncomfortable in the limelight. But he knew his job was on the line with this case. If he succeeded in solving the case and bringing the person responsible to justice, a promotion would be imminent.

He watched as the police divers headed out to sea. They knew the location in which the backpack had been found and researched the tides and winds. They had a search area mapped out. Bromley hoped the girl would be found even if it meant it was only her body that was recovered. At least they would have some answers.

At eight o'clock he decided to pop up and check on Jenkins and headed up Peninsula Road to Tiromoana. He noticed the wooden gate was closed at the entrance. He got out of the car and saw it was not bolted, just latched. He opened the gate and drove up the long tree lined driveway. As they reached the top of the driveway he observed a metal gate was also closed. He knew Audrey had sheep on the property due to the signage "Sheep – please close the gates." He duly opened the gate, drove through and closed it as requested.

There was no sign of Jenkins' car. *He must be out*, he thought. He decided to talk to Audrey. He had never actually met the lady and thought it was only polite to introduce himself and see if she knew where Jenkins was.

He walked around the front of the cottage. He could see it had originally been an old tin garage. It now had a bright red awning over the front sliding glass doors. The cottage had been freshly painted white with red trim. He guessed to match the awning. The gardens were well kept and the lawn freshly mown. All in all the property was well maintained and the view was spectacular. He could see across Doubtless Bay over to the Karikari Peninsula. The bay was spotted with police boats and divers. He knocked on the door and waited.

She must be here somewhere, he thought as he knocked again. Her car was parked at the top end of the gravel driveway. He recognized the Rav4. He walked around the cottage and over to the cabin. The curtains were pulled and he couldn't see inside.

He knocked and waited for a few minutes. When he got no response, he left the property and headed back down to the beach. He would try again later in the day. He really wanted to have another conversation with Jenkins.

CHAPTER 46

It was in the early hours of the morning when Audrey put all of Jenkins belongings in his car and tidied the cabin. She would do a full clean when she returned. She had stripped the bed and put all the linens in the washing machine in the cottage laundry. She wanted no evidence of Jenkins on her property. He had drawn too much attention to her and now it was time to take that attention away from her.

It had been more difficult to move Jenkins, however. It required another trip on her trusted dolly. She managed to get him into the passenger seat of his car and she drove off into the darkness making sure to close both gates behind her. Every detail was crucial to her plan.

At the end of the driveway Audrey turned left and headed up the peninsula. At the end of the peninsula was Berghans Point. Audrey had never ventured very far up the peninsula. At the end of the public road was private property that reached for miles. Audrey just had to find a remote area to leave the car and Gavin.

A few kilometers up the road she found the perfect place. It was off the road and out of sight.

She got out of the car and pulled Gavin into the driver's seat. She carefully removed his rifle from the back seat and placed it by the body. She made it fall from his head so it looked like a suicide. She was wearing gloves and had covered her boots and wore a hat to prevent any of her DNA from being found at the scene. She took her time making sure every detail was taken care of.

The most important detail was the girl's panties with the pink and purple hearts. She had neatly packed them in his bag knowing the police would search his belongings and there would be no doubt as to his connection with the missing girl.

As additional and final proof of his involvement in the girl's murder she had discovered a flash drive with photos of the girl. The photos proved Gavin Jenkins was an abomination. It was by pure chance she had discovered the small card. She had found it hidden in an inside pocket of his raincoat when she was looking for his cell phone. Obviously, the police had not discovered it there. She had taken the battery out of the phone and disposed of it in the dense bush on the side of the road.

It had taken more time than she expected to take care of business. She looked at her phone and saw it was getting on to seven thirty. The sun was already out and it was going to be a beautiful clear day. She knew she had to get down the peninsula and off the road before anyone stirred. Her neighbors were mostly retired and traffic on the road was little to none most of the time. She had plenty of time to duck into the bush if she heard a car. The road had not been tar sealed and the loose gravel was a good warning indicator.

She removed her protective gear when she reached her driveway and tucked them into her bag. There had not been a single car in sight. It was such a lovely morning she decided to continue walking down the road towards the Hihi beach. She was curious about what was happening on the beachfront and could hear activity down by the motor camp and presumed the police were preparing for a day of searching the bay.

When she reached the beach she was shocked at the huge crowd of on lookers and media. She passed the crowd and headed off towards the little lawn park on the other side of the beach. She could observe from there without being noticed. She saw Detective Sergeant Burt arrive and join the other police on the shore. A moment later the local Mangonui Police Constable arrived and was swarmed by the media. Police Divers were preparing for a day underwater.

She was about to leave when she saw the local police car heading up peninsula road. *Shit!* She thought. I bet he is going to my place to check on Jenkins. I know he still suspects him. Oh well, it won't do any harm. I might as well let it be known I am down here in case I need a witness or two. And, with that, Audrey walked over to the nearest group of on lookers and started a conversation.

"I live just up the road," she said. "I can't believe this is happening. I do hope they don't find her in the bay. How awful would that be?"

Her friendly approach encouraged a deluge of conversation. Before long she had made friends with the crowd and ensured they knew whom she was by the time the local police car returned to the beach.

Audrey smiled. Her plan was working just fine. She headed up the road thinking of what she would cook for breakfast. She had built up quite an appetite. Pancakes and a cup of tea sounded just perfect. After that she would air out the cabin and get it ready for the next guest. She would place the ad on Trade Me today. Life was looking up.

Chapter 47

Bruce Bromley was having a cuppa on his deck watching the activity in the bay. His nephew insisted they had it under control but he was itching to get out there. Years as a volunteer fireman had wet his appetite for dealing with emergencies.

He reached into his pocket and retrieved his old flip up cell phone and dialed his mates up the road. "Wanna come for a ride out into the bay and see if we can give a hand?" he asked. His mates were eager to oblige. They lived a couple of miles up the peninsula road and were ready, hats in hand, within thirty minutes.

The day was turning into a beauty. Bruce waved at the police boat anchored not far from his beach. They had divers in the water and Bruce stopped his boat to enquire if they could be of any help.

The police on board suggested they go further up the coast towards Berghans Point. Bruce and the guys had binoculars on board and as they neared the end of the peninsula they got to work. For an hour they scoured the rocky coastline. Steep cliffs protruded from the shoreline to the high ridge above. The water was crystal clear, exposing seaweed and a stony seabed.

At first it looked like a seal had been washed up against the rocks. An unusual shape covered in debris and seaweed could be seen in the far distance near the point. Bruce shouted out to the other guys and pointed.

"We may have found something!" he shouted as he steered the boat towards the point.

Before long the area was abuzz with police and helicopters. The media was filming from above. The police were scrambling across the rocks to the body. It was presumed to be Suzy Cunningham but until the body could be officially identified the media could only broadcast that a girl's body had been found at Berghams Point but had not yet been identified as the missing girl.

Constable Bromley had a body, which meant he possibly had a homicide on his hands. It would not be long before the cause of death would be known. He doubted any DNA would still be retrievable on the body after being in the water for so long. Maybe he was wrong. The Coroner would carry out a post-mortem examination to confirm cause of death. Hopefully forensics will be able to pick up something to assist with finding the person responsible.

He thought about his "persons of interest" list. At the moment it contained only one name, Gavin Jenkins. It was time to make that second visit to his cabin. As he drove the kilometer up the hill from the beach he thought about how many coincidences tied Jenkins to Suzy. Firstly, his car had been seen near where she disappeared. Secondly, Suzy's backpack was found floating two beaches along from where his cabin is located.

Thirdly, her body - if it is her body, was found on the same peninsula coastline. There were just too many coincidences. Jenkins was involved, he just had to prove it.

CHAPTER 48

Audrey expected the Constable to return. She was ready and waiting when she heard his patrol car drive up the driveway.

For the past two hours she had cleaned the cabin of all traces of Gavin. She had picked the first of the spring flowers and placed them in a bright colored jug in the center of the small wood table. The bed was freshly made with ironed linens and the woodwork was polished with sweet swelling oils. She had been quick to place the ad on Trade Me. She even had time to do a quick fix of the surrounding garden and sweep off the deck.

Audrey had thrown her boot covers and gloves in the fire and watched them burn. They were the last pieces of evidence that could tie her to Gavin's demise.

She saw the Constable go directly up to the Cabin and knock at the door. She waited knowing his next move would be to come to the cottage. She opened the door with a happy and welcoming smile.

"Constable Bromley," he introduced himself "Do you happen to know where Gavin Jenkins is? I see his car is missing."

"Oh, I am so sorry Constable, but I cannot help you. This morning I noticed his car gone and while he was out I decided to do his garden. Don't like to disturb the tenants, you see. And I noticed the curtains were not drawn and it looked as though his personal belongings were gone. I used my key to check inside and sure enough the wardrobe was empty and so were the dresser drawers. He had already paid a month's rent in advance so I have no cause to complain." Audrey rambled on happily.

"He didn't leave any message as to where he has gone, or why?" He asked looking frustrated.

"No, but you are most welcome to look inside the cabin" she offered. "Maybe you will find something I missed."

Audrey accompanied the constable over to the cabin and unlocked the door "I have placed an ad on Trade Me" she said. "I didn't expect to be advertising it again so soon."

"Nice place" said Bromley "I hear the fishing is good around here."

"It's great. I'll leave you to it. You know where to find me," she said and returned to the cottage.

Bromley paced up and down the small cabin. "Damn! Where can he have gone?" he said. "I will put out a trace on his car and bring him in for questioning. He has some explaining to do.

He walked over to the cottage and found Audrey sitting on a lounge chair staring out into the bay. "Sorry to disturb you again," he said. "I'll be on my way."

"Oh, please, it is no problem. I am happy to help in any way," said. "You don't think Gavin had anything to do with the girl's disappearance?" she asked.

"She is no longer missing," said Bromley. "Her body was found just an hour ago down by Berghams Point. Well, it hasn't been officially identified as Suzy Cunningham but we are pretty sure it is she. Please call me if Jenkins returns," he said handing her his card "It is very urgent that I speak with him."

"Of course," she replied.

Audrey watched him get into his car and drive away. She sighed as a sweet calmness washed over her. The body of Suzy Cunningham couldn't have surfaced at a more opportune time. It wouldn't be too long before they found his car and the deceased Gavin. She liked it when all the loose ends came together so perfectly.

It must be time for a glass of champagne. She looked at the time – it was two thirty. She should eat some cheese and biscuits as well. "Better not get too tipsy in the middle of the day."

CHAPTER 49

Paul Jamieson had just arrived in Mangonui and had booked a room in a quaint hotel on the waterfront. He chose it because it looked deserted. There was an Indian Restaurant next door but noticed a *"Closed for the Winter"* sign on the door. It didn't matter to him. He had not come for the food but to get away from the city and, more importantly, from a job he hated. His boss had accused him of embezzling funds from the company and he had a choice to either resign or be subject to a police interrogation. He chose the former and was looking forward to six months solitude and a chance to try his hand at writing a book. His Mother's death had resulted in a small inheritance providing funds for his much-needed getaway.

He promised himself no women, no getting wasted, no weed and no socializing until the book was finished. An occasional beer would be ok. In fact he felt like one right now. He walked down the waterfront and saw an old pub. The bar was deserted except for couple of old guys who looked like regulars. He nodded to them and they nodded back.

"How's it going?" one asked him.

"Great" he replied. "And you?"

"Can't complain" the man answered back.

The guys went back to their conversation. Paul could hear them as he sat at the bar only a few feet away.

"Can't believe they found her in the bay. Only sixteen she was. Real pretty girl. Shame."

Paul wondered what they were talking about. Sounded like a murder. Surely not in this small, quiet town. Then he remembered hearing something on the news about a missing redhead.

"Excuse me," he said. "Are you talking about the missing girl who was on the news? Have they found her?"

"Must be her," said one of the guys. "I guess they have to identify the body but who else would it be?"

"Real shame," said Paul.

They all agreed.

Paul asked if they knew of any place around he could rent that was nice and quiet.

The guys said they didn't. He finished his beer and decided to take a walk around the small village before heading back to his room. He needed to find a place soon. Somewhere out of the way. I'll check on Trade Me when I get back, he thought. It is winter and there should be somewhere local at a good price."

He thought about the girl found in the bay. "Could be just the story I am looking for. A real-life murder mystery." He hurried back to his hotel room to do some online research. *What luck*, he thought. *I just happened to arrive in a town when a girl is pulled out of the bay.*

CHAPTER 50

By the time Bromley had returned to the station the news was spreading fast. Social media was taking the place of newspapers and television now. It was more immediate and often more accurate. Police even used twitter to break news. Sometimes Bromley wished they could go back to when you had to wait until the six o'clock news or the morning newspaper to keep up with the news. Now it was instant. A news app on your mobile phone gave you instant access. Updates every second.

Detective Sergeant Burt had taken the girl's parents to identify the body. It was confirmed. It was Suzy. They released the news to the media. Bromley knew the Cunningham's would be devastated. He just couldn't bring himself to tell them what Suzy was doing at the Taipa Shopping Center that night. How could he? They already had to deal with the death of their beautiful daughter. Finding out she was prostituting herself would be just too much to handle. He wondered if he was holding off telling them because he felt guilty. Why didn't he know what his daughter was up to? She was with Suzy. Of course they would blame him. They had to blame someone.

Something was nagging at him. Ever since he had left Audrey's place he could feel it. Then he realized what it was. Why did Audrey place an ad on Trade Me to find a new tenant for the cabin? Jenkins had paid a month in advance. He might have just gone away for a few nights and packed up his things. He didn't have to tell his landlady where he was going. Did she know something he didn't? Did she know he wasn't coming back? How would she know? Had Jenkins told her he was leaving for good. Was he trying to evade the police and was she helping him?

He had put a trace on his car. He knew all the police in the surrounding areas were keeping an eye out for it. They would find him. He was sure of it.

As he was sitting at his desk the coroner called to give him the results of the girl's autopsy. She had been choked to death. The red blood vessels in the eyes indicated she had been smothered to death a few days ago. Most probably about the time she went missing. She had not drowned, as there was no sign of water in the lungs and had already been dead about twenty-four hours before she was dumped in the bay. Forensics was working on identifying any DNA that might be found in the girl's body. The results should be in a day or so.

Bromley knew now he definitely had a homicide on his hands. And he was pretty sure he knew who did it. Proving it was going to be another thing.

CHAPTER 51

Audrey was feeling pretty intoxicated when the phone rang. She hated answering the phone almost as much as she hated surprises and she cursed that her telephone didn't have caller ID. She considered letting it go to answerphone but changed her mind.

"Hello," she answered evasively.

"Hi," said a man's voice. "You have an ad on Trade Me. Is the cabin still available? If so, I would like to come and have a look at it."

Audrey liked his voice; so cultured, so refined. "Is it just for you?" she asked.

"Yes. I am looking for a quiet place to write for a few months." The man offered.

"As I mention in the ad I require a six month's minimum commitment," she said. "How long are you looking at?"

"Oh, six months is fine," he said. "I am just in Mangonui. Would it be OK to pop around now?"

Audrey gave him the directions and made a dash for the bathroom. She was not really looking her best. She brushed her unkempt hair and twirled it into a knot on the top of her head. She could make up her face in seconds... moisturizer, powder, blush, eye shadows, eyeliner, and mascara with red lipstick and gloss finish.

"There," she said admiring her quick fix. She changed into black stretch pants and her favorite v -neck black stretch top. After wrapping a black and white, soft scarf around her neck, she checked the result in her full-length mirror.

"It'll have to do," she said as she ran over to the cabin to turn on the lights and light a vanilla candle to freshen the air.

It was only a few minutes before she heard him coming up the drive. She walked outside the cabin and waved at him and pointed to the parking area. He was driving a black Range Rover. As he stepped out she felt her heart race and her knees weaken.

He was gorgeous! Dark, blonde hair, slight stubble, lean, strong, sexy body. He walked towards her smiling.

"You must be Audrey," he said.

Audrey wasn't usually lost for words. Communication was something she excelled at. She felt like a silly schoolgirl as she ushered him inside the brightly lit cabin.

"This is great!" the man said. Oh, by the way I am Paul Jamieson. I would really like to take it." Getting no response, he continued on. "I have references. I am quite reputable."

"Oh, I'm sure you are," Audrey said while thinking, and you have beautiful hazel eyes.

"Can I take it?" he asked.

"When do you want to move in?"

"Tomorrow, if that is alright." He replied. "I will email you my references when I get back to the hotel."

Audrey was surprised at her instant attraction for this man. It had been many, many years since a man made her feel like this. In fact, she could only think of one time and that was over thirty years ago. But that was another time. This was now and her life was different now.

"That would be fine," she said. What time do you think you will be moving in?"

"About ten if that's OK."

"Feel free to have a wander around the property," she said. "Just follow the sign to the road that leads to the beach. It is a great fishing spot." There is also a path along the ridge in front of the cottage to the other beach. I will see you at ten." And she left him to explore.

When Audrey returned to the cottage she was literally quivering. He had everything she ever wanted in a man; elegance, sexuality, strength, great body, intelligence, wonderful voice; she could go on. She felt wonderful.

CHAPTER 52

Bruce Bromley answered the phone.

"Hey Jimmy," he said, "I wondered when you would call."

"Just wanted to touch base and say thanks for all your help today. There is no doubt it is Suzy Cunningham, and it would appear to be a homicide," said his nephew.

"Was she drowned?" Bruce asked.

"No, she was dead before going into the bay. She was asphyxiated. Seems too coincidental that you found both the backpack and the body close to the Hihi peninsula," said Bromley.

"I have been thinking the same thing," said Bruce. "You think it is that Jenkins guy, don't you?"

"If it smells like a rat, it usually is a rat" The policeman responded." I went to talk with him this afternoon and he has already checked out - gone. Must have known we were on to him."

"Gone? When did he leave?" Asked Bruce.

"Audrey said he was gone when she got up this morning. She has already advertised the place for a new tenant."

"Audrey said he was gone this morning? That's strange. I saw her going over to the cabin all dolled up with a bottle of wine about nine-ish last night. They must have had a lover's tiff."

"You were spying on them?"

"Well, yes. I was curious. I suspected Jenkins and just went over for a look to see what he was up to. He seemed pretty pleased to see her. But I couldn't get too close so I don't know what they were talking about. I left shortly after she went inside the cabin."

"I wonder why Audrey never mentioned their little evening get together."

"You don't think she could be involved do you?" asked Bruce.

"No, never. She doesn't seem that calculating. Pretty much an open book. Maybe you misread her intentions. She could have just been neighborly. But, as you seem to be finding every piece of evidence, let me know if you see Jenkins car anywhere will you?"

"Absolutely. I'll pass the word around. But I would think he would be long gone by now."

As soon as he hung the phone Bruce called out to Marge. "Hey Marge, you haven't seen Jenkins' silver Toyota since last night have you?"

Bruce had filled Marge in of the latest details and she was intrigued to say the least. She had been full of questions and had been on the phone with her friends most of the morning relaying the latest news.

The whole area was shocked. Finding the missing girl in the bay. Now they know it is Suzy Cunningham's body and she was murdered, the police will be swarming the area searching for Jenkins.

Marge walked inside wearing gardening gloves. "Is it the Cunningham girl?" she enquired. "Do they know yet?"

"Yes, it is. And it looks like murder. I can't believe it may have happened right here in Hihi. I think I will ring the boys up the road and see if they have seen Jenkins' car anywhere. In fact I will take a drive up the peninsula and have a look around. Although I can't imagine that he would still be around here. He must be south of Auckland by now."

Marge agreed and went back to spraying copper on their fruit trees. Marge loved to garden and her fruit trees were her pride and joy. Plum chutney, plum jam, peach jam, peach preserves; she sold them at the Taipa Market.

CHAPTER 53

Every television in Northland was tuned to the six o'clock news.

"The missing girl, Suzy Cunningham's body was found this morning in Doubtless Bay close to Berghans point only one or two kilometers from where her back pack was found yesterday. It has been confirmed by the police, working on the case, the cause of death was asphyxiation. Indicating she was dead before entering the bay. The police are considering the death a homicide and are requesting any information the public may have in the case to contact the Mangonui Police Station. They are also looking for a person of interest, Gavin Jenkins, and his car a silver Toyota Celica license number AZQ1459. If anyone knows the whereabouts of Mr. Jenkins or his car please contact the Police with the information."

They showed shots from the helicopter circling Berghams Point where they discovered the body. A picture of the pretty redhead was on the screen. A photo of Jenkins' silver Toyota was also shown.

The Cunningham's were seated on their sofa surrounded by

family. Mark and Betty were inconsolable. Their grief was profound. Betty kept moaning over and over again. "My little girl, my little girl. Why? Why? Who would murder my sweet girl?" Constable Bromley had called on them earlier to tell them the news that they were considering it a homicide.

Mark asked the family if they knew this guy, Jenkins? He couldn't understand why the police were looking for a man in his fifties in relation to the murder. Constable Bromley had said they were interested in talking to him again because he had been seen near the Taipa Shopping Center where Suzy went missing. Mark had understood that they had already searched Jenkins' cabin and they found nothing. Now the constable had told him Jenkins had gone missing. Checked out of the cabin with no explanation or forwarding address. The police found this suspicious. Was he responsible for his daughter's murder?

CHAPTER 54

It was just after the six o'clock news when a woman called and left a message for Constable Bromley saying she was Gavin Jenkins' sister. Bromley returned the call as soon as he received the message.

"Constable Bromley here from the Mangonui Police. You left me a message?"

"Yes. My name is Diane Jenkins. I am Gavin Jenkins' sister. I understand my brother is missing."

"That is correct. He was staying at a cabin in Hihi and we talked to him yesterday. However, today when we went by to ask him to come to the station for some further questioning, he had checked out of the cabin and left no forwarding address. Is he with you? Have you heard from him?

"No. I knew nothing about this until I heard it on the news. He is not with me. I can't imagine where he is. I am worried about him. It is not like him to just take off. Why are you questioning him about the murdered girl?" His sister asked.

"He was just helping us with our enquiries," said Bromley. "He was seen near where the girl went missing."

"If he is missing, there is something terribly wrong," she said. "He is a kind, gentle man. He would not hurt a fly." I have tried calling him on his cell but it just goes to voice mail." I am coming up. I should be there in about four hours. I will book myself into the Mangonui hotel. I'll call you in the morning."

"Can you give me his cell phone number?" said Bromley.

Diane gave him the number and agreed to notify the police if she heard from him. She was distraught. Bromley was surprised by her reaction. Maybe his disappearance is suspect. Did he commit the crime and drive his car off a cliff somewhere? He notified the police crews to look for a possible suicide. You never know and it pays to cover all the bases.

Something was not quite right. Why did Audrey not tell him they shared a drink last night in his cabin? What was going on?

He decided to make a telephone call to Audrey. She had some explaining to do.

CHAPTER 55

Paul is sitting at the bar at the hotel. He just finished a wonderful dinner at the Thai Restaurant in the village and was enjoying a beer before settling in for the night. He was looking forward to moving into the cabin tomorrow. Nice place, nice lady. It's the perfect writer's retreat. He would begin to do some research tonight online and see what he could find out about the murdered girl found in the bay.

He saw her walk in - a large lady with long blonde hair. She joined him at the bar and ordered a Vodka and Tonic. She looked upset.

"Nice evening," said Paul being friendly.

"I hadn't noticed," she replied.

"You look a little troubled, if I may say so," he said.

"I have just driven here from Auckland. I have been going like a bat out of hell. My brother is missing," she confided, wondering why she was telling a complete stranger her problems.

"When did he go missing?" he asked.

"The police said he has been missing since last night."

"The Police!" Paul said surprised. "Why are the police looking for him?"

"They think he may know something about the girl who was found murdered in Hihi bay," she said in a whisper.

"Your brother is Gavin Jenkins?" he said surprised.

"Yes. I am Diane Jenkins. He rented a little cabin in Hihi and had just moved in about a week ago and the police said this morning he just left without telling the landlady. It is not like him. I am worried."

"A cabin in Hihi. Paul asked in shock.

"Yes, I found it for him on Trade Me. It sounded nice and Gavin loves to fish and it had a private road to a fishing beach.

"I am moving into a cabin in Hihi tomorrow." Said Paul. "It sounds like the same one. Do you want to come with me and ask the landlady if your brother stayed there?   And, if so, if she knows where he went? Maybe she didn't want to confide in the police for some reason. I am sure your brother is OK. Most probably just gone off on a fishing trip somewhere."

"Oh, I hope you are right. And yes I would love to come with you tomorrow. What time?" Diane asked.

"I plan to move in about ten. You can follow me in your car. By the way my name is Paul Jamieson. Pleased to meet you," he said offering his hand. "I am in Room ten. Call me about quarter to ten in the morning and we will head up there." Paul stood up. "I have some work to do, I'll see you in the morning." He left the bar and headed off to his room.

Paul was curious and decided to Google his new landlady. He typed in *Audrey Wetherby, Northland, New Zealand* - the name on the email address on Trade Me. He got a hit. Apparently, Audrey owned The Three Suites in Whangaroa and there had been a couple of murders in the area only last year. Two middle-aged men stayed at The Three Suites in the same unit before they were found murdered in the area. Could that be the same Audrey Wetherby? He wondered.

He searched for more information on the murdered men and found a person had been arrested for the crimes. "Damn," he said. "I thought she might have been the killer. I must be losing it."

He then searched for information on the Cunningham case. Reports by the police said she had been asphyxiated before going into the water. A silver Toyota had been seen near the Taipa shopping center where the girl was last seen alive.

What was the girl doing there? He wondered. *Did Jenkins stay in the very same cabin that he was moving into tomorrow?* He would find out soon enough now he had a contact on the inside. Diane Jenkins was coming with him tomorrow.

He stayed up until the wee hours creating a list of questions that needed to be answered. Then turned out the light and fell immediately to sleep.

CHAPTER 56

A udrey had heard the six o'clock news and knew the
police had found the bloody girl and knew it was
murder. If they were looking for Jenkins in relation
to the murder she must help them find him – and quickly. If
word got out in the media that the man had been staying at her
place then shit would hit the fan. Eventually they would look
into her background. She knew she had some skeletons in her
closet and it would not do to have them exposed.

The phone rang and she had a feeling she shouldn't answer it.
But thought it might be Paul asking her something about the
cabin and she didn't want to lose him now.

"Hello," she answered.

"Constable Bromley here. Sorry to disturb you but I have a
couple of questions for you. Is this a good time?"

Fuck! Thought Audrey. She used her soft, welcoming voice
and said "Certainly Constable anything I can do to help. I heard
you found the girl's body today. How awful."

"We really need to talk to Jenkins and, as you were the last
person to see him, I thought you may be of help." Bromley said.

"I guess I was," said Audrey thinking on her feet. "What questions do you have?"

"When was the last time you saw Jenkins?" He asked.

Audrey wondered why he was asking this question. Did he know she had drinks with him last night? "Last night about nine o'clock," she answered.

"Where was he then?" he asked.

"Oh, in his cabin," she said.

"So you saw him in his cabin last night?"

"Yes, I dropped a bottle of wine over to him as a welcome gift. I shared a glass with him and then returned to my cottage.

"What time was that?"

"About nine thirty or maybe earlier," she said.

"Well that answers my question... Oh one more thing. Why are you advertising the cabin so soon? Maybe Jenkins has just gone on a fishing trip somewhere. You said he paid a month in advance?"

Audrey knew she was cornered. She wanted to eliminate any doubts and this was the time to do it.

"Well," she said. "I didn't want to say anything but after what Gavin told me that night, I just knew he was not coming back."

"What did he tell you?" he asked.

Audrey paused. This was it. "He seemed troubled, depressed even. I asked him what was wrong. At first he wouldn't say anything but after a couple of drinks he told me he had a lot on his mind and when I pressed him further he got annoyed and asked me to leave. I noticed that he had emptied his wardrobe and had a couple of travel bags open on the bed. I asked him if he was going somewhere. He said, "What do you care? I have already paid you a month's rent – you can keep it. I didn't know what he meant by that until I noticed he had taken all his belongings the next morning."

"Where do you think he was going?" he asked.

"I don't know," she said. "But I have been thinking" she paused and took a deep breath. "Last night I thought I heard a gunshot. It was about eleven o'clock. I was watching a movie on television. I was worried Gavin may have done something, and I went over to the cabin, but the lights were all out and there wasn't any sign of him. I did look inside and saw the cabin was empty. I presumed he had gone out and I went back to bed. Now I think the shot came from up the peninsula somewhere. Maybe he drove up there. I just don't know. It is most probably nothing at all. But I thought I should tell you. Maybe someone else heard the shot too. One of the neighbors."

The constable said he would check on it and thanked her for her cooperation.

Audrey hung up the phone and smiled. Surely, they will carry out a search tomorrow up the peninsula and find Gavin. With the panties and the flash drive in his suitcase and his gun by his side she felt confident Constable Bromley would know he had his man.

She wasn't going to let anything spoil her morning tomorrow. Audrey headed off into the bathroom to have a long hot soak in a bubble bath. She would dye her hair tonight and get up early and make herself look gorgeous for the arrival of her new, sexy tenant. She found herself singing in the bath. Life was great.

CHAPTER 57

Diane didn't get much sleep. She was worried about her brother. *I should have let him stay with me,* she thought. *It was my idea to send him up here to live in the middle of nowhere and now he is missing.*

She sat at her computer searching everything she could find on the girl's murder. She also checked online for the Trade Me ad for the cabin but it was nowhere to be found. She guessed it had been taken off now that it was rented. She was hoping to find out the name of the landlady. She couldn't remember the name on the ad she had given Gavin. But she would recognize the cabin once she got there.

Diane always felt like a slender woman and was constantly shocked by her reflection in a mirror or a shop window. Most of her life she had been admired by men. She had always taken her nice figure and long hair for granted. Then suddenly she became hungry. The hunger would not go away resulting in the size she was today. At least she was invisible now. The larger she became the more invisible she became. No one admired her or looked her way.

She enjoyed her singular lifestyle and recently had developed an insatiable appetite for collecting things. At first it was books, magazines and newspapers but over the past few months she had added clothes to the mix. Being overweight prevented her from shopping in store so she shopped online. Only trouble was, it was too easy and it had become an obsession. She was a regular customer on Trade Me. Hence finding the cabin ad for Gavin.

She looked at her watch for the tenth time this morning. Finally, it was quarter to ten and time to call Paul. He answered the phone and said he would meet her out the front of the hotel. He just had to check out. She had booked her room for a couple of nights hoping she would find where Gavin was by then. Diane was wearing a navy-blue flowing skirt with a matching blue jacket and blue and white scarf. She hated wearing high heels and had opted for a pair of black boots.

Paul was true to his word. He was parked not far from Diane's car. Paul led the way out of the village up to the ten highway and took the Hihi turnoff. It was about a ten-minute drive. As they passed Hihi beach Diane looked across the bay and felt really sad for the poor girl who they had found there. It was a gravel road up the peninsula and before long she was following Paul down a long driveway.

As soon as they reached the cabin she knew it was the same one. She took a deep breath. Why had Gavin left here? Where had he gone? She wondered. The landlady must have known he wasn't coming back or she wouldn't have rented the cabin to Paul.

CHAPTER 58

The media were like hounds. Newspapers and television reporters from all over the country had gathered into the small town of Mangonui. Bromley looked out the window and decided getting out of the station without being mauled would be a challenge. It was eight o'clock and he had a press conference scheduled for nine. Detective Burt had been overseeing the search and was going to address the media with him. There was no new information since last night so he imagined the interviews were going to be short and sweet. He needed to get up to the peninsula and make sure Jenkins had not driven off a cliff. Surely Audrey was overreacting. He called his uncle to ask if he had heard any shots a couple of nights ago. If Audrey heard a gunshot he was sure Bruce would have heard it too.

"Bruce" he said as he answered the phone. "Jimmy here again. I was talking with Audrey last night and she mentioned hearing a gunshot a couple of nights ago. I don't suppose you heard anything?"

"Funny that," said Bruce. "I did hear a shot. Thought it was pig shooters. You know the pig shooting competition is running at the moment."

"Do you remember what time?" he asked.

"Just after the ten thirty news. Must have been about eleven or so. I remember because I had just turned off the tele as I always do after the news. Why? Has something happened?"

"No, nothing. Just wanted to follow up. Thanks Bruce."

Constable Bromley hung up the phone in deep thought. Maybe Audrey was right. He knew Jenkins had a gun. He arranged with the dog handler to meet him at the Hihi motor camp at ten thirty. He heard Detective Burt walk into the station and called him into his office to discuss the latest development. They agreed not to notify the media of their suspicions until they had some concrete evidence. The two walked outside to address the frenetic crowd. A young lady thrust her microphone into Bromley's face and said "We have received a tip that Suzy Cunningham was an under aged prostitute and was working under the name of Red. Was she working the night she went missing?"

"At this time we can only confirm that Suzy Cunningham's body was retrieved from Doubtless Bay near Berghams Point. Her death has been confirmed as a homicide. We are pursuing all leads associated with her death. At this time we do not have a suspect. We ask the public, if they have any information relating to the case, to please contact the nearest police station. Thank you."

Detective Burt and Constable Bromley had agreed to not divulge any information regarding the girl's illegal prostitution activities. Obviously, her parents had no idea she was leading a double life. However, now that the press had got hold of the information they knew they must talk to the Cunningham's sooner than later. After that they would head up to the Hihi peninsula to join the search.

Chapter 59

It was ten o'clock on the dot when she heard Paul's car coming up the driveway. She was surprised to see another car pull in behind his. She had believed he was alone up here and wondered who it could possibly be. She watched as a large, blonde women stepped out of her car and walked over to Paul. They appeared to be deep in conversation. The woman was obviously very agitated. Audrey didn't want to interrupt their conversation and decided to wait until they approached her.

A few minutes later there was a knock at her door. Audrey went to greet her new tenant and was introduced to Diane Jenkins. It was unexpected and quite disturbing to Audrey to realize this woman was Gavin's sister. How the hell did she find Peter and why were they together?

Peter soon explained, "I met her at the hotel last night and she had mentioned her brother was staying at a cabin in Hihi. We thought it might be your cabin so she followed me up here."

"It is this cabin," said Diane "Where is he? He told me he was pleased with the cabin and was planning on staying here long-term. Why would he leave? He said he was happy here."

"I am so sorry," said Audrey calmly. Your brother is a really nice guy. Although I didn't really get to know him well. He was only here for just over a week. I did talk to him the night before he left and he seemed distraught, depressed and I noticed he was packing. He wouldn't tell me what was wrong and got annoyed when I asked him if he was going somewhere."

"Did he say he wasn't coming back?" Diane asked accusingly.

"No, but he took everything from the cabin. He had unpacked all his belonging into drawers and into the wardrobe and when I went into the cabin the next morning everything was gone. It was obvious he wasn't coming back. I think he was running from something or someone," she added. "He seemed agitated - afraid even."

"My brother had nothing to be afraid of. He lived a simple life. Why would he be afraid? Do you know something?" asked Diane getting agitated herself.

"Maybe Audrey will let you look inside the cabin and see if you can see anything of Gavin's belongings. Would you mind, Audrey?" asked Paul.

"No, of course I don't mind," said Audrey graciously. "Please look in the cabin. I can tell you there is nothing there. But if it makes you feel better - go ahead. Here is the key," she handed Paul the key.

The two headed off towards the cabin. Diane was now in tears. Paul was comforting her. Audrey was pissed. This morning was not going as she expected. She wanted Paul all to herself. Now he was acting the big protector of Diane. Bloody woman! Why did she have to find her and the cabin? Well, she would soon find out where her precious brother was. She hoped the police were doing a search of the peninsula - she had given them enough clues. Where the hell were they. She hadn't heard a single car coming up the isolated road except of course for Paul and Diane.

She watched out her back window at the two of them walking around the cabin. She had left the cabin curtains open to let the morning sun in. It was a beautiful day. Cool but sunny. Blue skies with wisps of white, fluffy clouds. The bay was glistening in the sunlight.

"Why did that fat women have to come and spoil it?" she murmured to herself.

Diane walked out to her car and Paul followed her. Audrey could see them talking. Diane was obviously pissed off. She got into her car and took off down the driveway. Paul reached into his Range Rover and removed a couple of bags and went back into the cabin. Audrey decided to keep her distance. She didn't want to begin their relationship with Gavin's disappearance being the main topic of conversation. She would wait until he settled in. She would go over at sunset and invite him over for a glass of wine on the front lawn.

CHAPTER 60

Bromley's conversation with the Cunningham's was a disaster. They were adamant that their daughter was not selling her body for money. "She was a good girl," they kept telling him. "We would have known if she was out on the streets prostituting herself."

There was no way Bromley could convince them otherwise. They had asked for proof and he had explained that Staci had told them Suzy was working the night she went missing.

"She is lying!" said Betty Cunningham. "I knew that girl was no good. She is making up stories. Have you asked your Lucy? Does she think Suzy is a prostitute?"

"We received an anonymous tip a couple of days ago confirming she was working the streets. However, this cannot be verified. We were not going to tell you until we had actual proof but it would appear that the media has got hold of this information and may release it to the public. We wanted to make sure you heard it from us first.

Mark and Betty were horrified. "They can't do that. They

can't ruin my poor girl's reputation. She is dead for God's sake." Betty wailed. "Can't you stop them?"

"We did not confirm their allegations, but we cannot prevent them from releasing the information if they can substantiate it" he replied.

"Well, I am sure they have no proof of such a thing? Said Bruce.

Detective Burt and Constable Bromley left the Cunningham's and headed off to the Hihi Peninsula. It was almost ten thirty and they wanted to lead the search.

Upon their arrival at the motor camp the police dog team greeted them. The dog and his handler headed up the peninsula road. The road had been blocked off and only residents were allowed access. A small group of local residents were already congregating by the camp. It wouldn't be long before the media caught on. Detective Burt kept a couple of officers by the camp to safeguard the area.

By eleven thirty the search team had made their way almost three kilometers up the road. Bromley was beginning to doubt his instincts but insisted they kept going.

At noon Bromley was just about to call off the search when he heard the dog barking. He ran to where the search team had gathered and saw the silver Toyota parked not far from the road. It was in a wooded area surrounded by tea tree and gorse. Detective Burt reached the car before Bromley and said, "We've found him. He's dead." He put on a pair of protective gloves and opened the driver's door. "Look like he was shot in the head." They radioed the forensics team and the coroner and waited for their arrival. The search team returned down peninsula road to a deluge of media. "No comment" they said as they pushed their way through the crowd.

It was mid-afternoon before the body and the car had been removed from the scene. There had been no doubt that Jenkins had been shot. Was it a suicide? Was it a homicide? They wouldn't have long to wait for the answer.

Bromley got the message about five thirty. Jenkins' finger-prints were the only ones found on the gun. There were no other fingerprints found in or on the car. His belongings were also searched. The forensics team had a question. "Was Suzy wearing a pair of panties with pink and purple hearts on them? A pair matching this description was found among Jenkins' personal items. They were processing them for DNA. There was also a flash drive found in his suitcase. They were sending the photos via email over to Bromley now.

Constable Bromley clicked on the photo attachments and sat in shock as he reviewed Jenkins' photos of Suzy. They were disturbing and confirmed Jenkins had been with the girl the night she went missing. They were damning proof. The girl was handcuffed, blind folded and at times even gagged.

It was time to call the Cunningham's. It was not going to be an easy conversation. But Bromley had to find out if the panties belonged to Suzy. If so, then they obviously had the killer and the case would be closed.

Constable Bromley hung up the phone and sighed. They had just confirmed his worse fears. Jenkins had obviously kept the girl's panties as a memento.

His next phone call was to the local hotel to talk to Jenkins' sister. Detective Burt has already taken Diane to the coroner's office to officially identify the body. She had broken down and sobbed uncontrollably. Bromley wanted to extend his condolences and ask her to come into the station tomorrow to answer a few questions if she was up to it. The hotel advised she had checked out.

He made it home in time to watch the six o'clock news. Suzy Cunningham's murder was the first story.

CHAPTER 61

The conversation between Diane and Audrey was still worrying Paul. He, too, couldn't understand why Diane's brother had left so suddenly and without any explanation. Could he believe Audrey? She had a history of being involved with missing, murdered, middle-aged men. He had not told Diane about the information he had found on Audrey. No need to cause her more grief, he thought. He just hoped this was not a murder too or there might be more to the sweet talking, innocent Audrey.

Paul unpacked his clothes and placed his laptop computer on the small wooden table. He had already asked Audrey about a wireless service and she had given him the password so he could access it. The signal was not very strong - but adequate. After checking his emails, he continued to research the Suzy Cunningham case. Diane had told him she planned on talking to the police, if she couldn't find her brother before tomorrow. She was going to call around his small circle of friends this afternoon. Maybe one of them had heard from him. Suzy Cunningham's Facebook page gave him access to her list of friends. He wondered if Lucy Bromley was any relation to Constable Bromley. It would appear Lucy was one of Suzy's closest friends. There were numerous photos of them both. Some of Suzy's photos looked a little too sexy for a sixteen-year-old. He did a search for Lucy Bromley. There was no record on Facebook or other social media sites. *That's strange,* he thought.

He had heard a dog barking up the peninsula about noon and wondered what a dog was doing in the area. The peninsula was a dedicated kiwi zone with strict rules prohibiting cats and dogs. The cabin was quite a distance from the road. Paul figured that they didn't take the "no dog" law very seriously.

At three o'clock Paul decided to take a walk down peninsula road to the Hihi beach. He hoped the small shop at the motor camp would be open so he could pick up some supplies.

It was a nice stroll downhill all the way. The rural road was lined in old pine trees, pungas and tea trees. There was thick bamboo on the corner before he reached the flats. Some shoots were precariously hanging over the road. The road continued around a few bends bordering the bay. It was full tide and the swollen bay crashed against the rocks on the shore.

Paul decided he should take this walk every day. It helped clear his head and give him time to structure the outline of his book.

Suddenly, he heard the crunching of car tires on the road behind him. He quickly stepped to one side to allow the vehicles through. He was taken back when he watched the St John's Ambulance and a police car pass him by and head down towards Hihi beach. He wondered why the ambulance did not have its siren on. Usually that indicated the person in the ambulance was deceased. For a quiet town it certainly had a lot happening.

When he reached the motor camp he saw a number of television vans pulling out and heading for the highway. A few locals were milling around the camp. He stopped and asked an elderly couple if they knew what was going on.

"They must have found that Jenkins man," a slender, well spoken, elderly lady informed him. "They had police dogs searching all morning up the peninsula. Then we saw an ambulance go up and come down."

"What makes you think it is the Jenkins guy?" Paul asked.

"Because we were talking to the television crew and that's what they told us," she replied.

Paul could see the shop was closed. 'Closed for the winter'the sign on the door read.

"Damn" said Paul. "I guess I will have to go into Mangonui for supplies."

"This is a holiday town," said the elderly man. "Only a few of us stay during the winter."

Paul sat on the park bench and looked out across the bay to the open sea in the far distance. He had heard a meteor originally formed Doubtless Bay. It certainly looked like an enormous crater with Karikari peninsula on one side and the Hihi Peninsula on the other.

On his way back to the cabin he wondered if it was Jenkins they had found. Should he call Diane at the hotel? He decided he would not upset her in case it wasn't Jenkins after all. He remembered she was going to visit the Mangonui Police today anyway.

Paul decided to wait until tomorrow to do his shopping. He had a couple of beers and a couple of steak pies that would last him until then.

By quarter to six the sun was beginning to set and Audrey was knocking at his door. "Shit! What the hell does she want?" He opened the door and saw her standing there all dressed up. "Yes?" he enquired.

"It is going to be such a wonderful sunset," she said.

"I have a couple of glasses and a bottle of wine on the front lawn and thought you might like to join me for a welcome drink."

"Sorry, but I was just settling in to watch the news. Another time," he said politely.

"Oh, OK then. Another time," she said.

He could see the light disappear from her green eyes. Her warm smile didn't vary. As he closed the door she turned on her heels and walked determinedly towards the cottage.

Paul turned on the news and watched in horror as he listened to the Suzy Cunningham update. Detective Burt was reading a statement to the press:

"Today we located the body of Gavin Jenkins. It would appear Mr. Jenkins took his own life. We have reason to believe that he was involved in Suzy Cunningham's murder. However, it is an ongoing investigation but we are not looking for any other suspect at this time. Suzy Cunningham's body was found in Doubtless Bay yesterday. She was sixteen years old. Our thoughts and prayers go out to her family and friends. We thank the public for their support."

"Poor Diane" he said. "I must call her and give her my condolences. She is here all alone and must be devastated. He dialed the number at the hotel and asked for Diane Jenkins. He was told she had checked out of the hotel and had given no forwarding address or left any message for him. He would wait and contact her tomorrow. Everyone can be located now either through social media or online directories.

He looked over at the lights in the cottage. He didn't know what to make of his landlady. She seemed to bring death with her wherever she goes. He would need to keep a safe distance from her.

While he is Mangonui tomorrow he might stop by the police station and talk to the officer in charge of Suzy's case. He was curious why they thought Jenkins was responsible for the murder. He also wanted to ask them about Audrey and the two murders over in Whangaroa last year. Both murdered men were also her guests. It seemed too much of a coincidence to ignore. He would tell him he had just moved into the cabin and wanted to make sure his life wasn't in jeopardy.

CHAPTER 62

Audrey watched the news with relief. They had found Gavin's body in his car and suspected suicide. The police were not looking for anyone else in relation to the murder. She was off the hook. There would be no reason for the police to contact her any more.

She had been disappointed that Paul preferred to watch the news rather than join her for a glass of champagne. She was hoping she could have distracted him. He already knew that Jenkins had stayed in his cabin and now his body was found just up the road she was worried he might decide to leave.

Audrey wondered what Paul was writing about. She had meant to ask him. If it weren't for that dreadful woman she would have had some alone time with Paul and would have learned more about him. She wondered if he had been married. Maybe he was married and just needed time away to write his book. He didn't appear to have much in the way of luggage. Maybe he had a home and family tucked away somewhere. She hoped not. Audrey wanted Paul all to herself.

She decided to have an early night and ran a hot bath laying out her pyjamas and warm dressing gown on the bed. She had just climbed into the bath and stretched out into the hot water when she heard the phone. "Bloody Hell!" she complained as she climbed back out of the bath to answer it.

"Hello" she snapped into the phone.

"Audrey?"

"Yes, who is it?"

"It's Diane Jenkins. I need to talk to you."

"I'm taking a bath. Can you call back later?" she said.

"O.K. I'll call you back," replied Diane.

Audrey stepped back into the bathtub. She used her toes to turn on the tap and refill it with hot water. The bath felt wonderful. 'Bloody woman" she complained. "Who does she think she is? First, she accuses me of what- I have no idea and then she needs to talk to me. I don't think so. I certainly won't be answering the phone tonight."

As Audrey climbed into bed and turned her electric blanket down to one, she heard the phone ringing again. Ignoring the call, she turned on the tele and listened to a movie until she fell asleep.

There was a noise outside Audrey's window. A rustling in the night. Eyes were watching.

CHAPTER 63

Constable Bromley decided to make Mary and the girls breakfast this morning. He was celebrating having solved the case. Well at least he had the killer and just had to tie up the loose ends. Bromley liked to cook. He popped in the toast as he checked the bacon, tomatoes and eggs sizzling in the fry pan. His wife had fallen for the infomercial on the stone non- stick fry pan. It was only non-stick the first two times you used it. He always had trouble turning over the eggs. The coffee pot sat on the table. One of his favorite aromas was the smell of bacon cooking, it reminded him of his youth.

He called the girls and went to wake up his wife. It is going to be a wonderful day today, he thought as he kissed his wife on her cheek.

Mary stirred and smiled. She could smell breakfast cooking and knew her husband must be in a good mood this morning. "What's the occasion?" she asked.

"Just celebrating life," he answered.

As the family sat down for breakfast they could hear the morning news on the television in the next room.

"There has been a new development in the Suzy Cunning-ham's murder case," the announcer was saying. "It has been confirmed by various sources that Suzy was better known as Red, a local prostitute working the streets at only sixteen years of age. This morning in the studio we have with us a man who does not want to be identified who will testify that Suzy Cunningham was prostituting herself at the Taipa Shopping Center on various separate occasions."

The news went on with the man's interview. He said he had seen her only a week before at the shopping center and a few times prior to that.

Bromley was furious. How dare the media destroy the young girl's reputation when she died such an awful death. *Oh God,* he thought. *Her parents – they will be devastated.*

He walked into the living room and stood in front of the TV and watched as the announcer said "Now we have an interview with Gavin Jenkins' sister."

He watched shocked as Diane Jenkins appeared on the screen.

"My brother is innocent," she said. "He did not kill himself. He was murdered. This is a conspiracy. That girl was a prostitute. Any man could have picked her up that night. It was not my brother. He was a quiet, respected man." She began to sob.

"Shit!" Bromley said. "I have to go to the station." All hell is breaking loose. Sorry about that. I'll see you later. He left his breakfast uneaten sitting on the kitchen table, surrounded by four forlorn faces.

CHAPTER 64

There were only a handful of television stations on the Freeview in the cabin. Paul tuned into TV One to watch the morning news. He wasn't disappointed. The story was getting bigger every day. If Suzy Cunningham was an under aged pro then Jenkins must have been her john on the night she was murdered. He hoped it hadn't happened in the bed he was sleeping in. The thought gave him the shudders.

He was surprised to see Diane talking about her brother. Didn't she realize the cops must have some proof he was responsible for her death or they wouldn't have announced it? But then, it is always difficult for family to accept their loved one could be a monster. He changed his mind about calling Diane. She obviously was coping with his death the best way she could, even if it was in complete denial.

He decided to get some writing done before he headed into Mangonui to do his grocery shopping. He needed to get everything down in writing while it was fresh in his mind. He was pleased Audrey had left freshly ground coffee and a small jug of milk in the fridge. There was also sugar and some condiments in the cupboard. It would keep him going until he hit the town for lunch.

It wasn't long before he heard Audrey's car going down the driveway. He wondered where she was going. She sounded like she was in a hurry. He kept typing and was soon lost in a writer's daze.

He jumped as he heard a knock at the door. He wasn't expecting anyone to be around and hadn't heard a car pulling up. It frightened the shit out of him. He pulled open the curtains on the sliding door and saw a short balding man facing him.

"So sorry to disturb you," said the man "I am looking for Audrey. Do you know if she is around?"

"I heard her leaving in her car about thirty minutes ago," he said.

"Damn," he swore. "You must be the new tenant. I'm your neighbor, Bruce Bromley. I live just over there," he said, pointing north across the lawn.

Paul recognized the name as the guy who found the backpack and the body. He had been reading an article online about how he, Bruce Bromley, was out in his boat during the search. He was an ex-firefighter and well known in the area.

"Pleased to me you. Paul Jamieson," he introduced himself. "There has been a lot going on around here."

"Bloody right there," Bruce said.

"You found the girl's body" Paul said, "That must have been difficult."

"Terrible, terrible," he said.

"Did you meet Gavin Jenkins who was staying in this cabin?" Paul enquired.

"No. Can't say I did. And a good thing too. Shocking what he did to that girl."

"Would you like a cup of coffee? I haven't got much else to

offer, as I haven't picked up any supplies yet. Just moved in yesterday afternoon," Paul explained.

"Don't mind if I do," said Bruce as he followed Paul to the small kitchen table.

"I'll just move my laptop and make more room," he said. "I am a writer and am taking a few months off to write a book. In fact, you might be just the man to help me get it off the ground."

"Why me?" asked Bruce.

"I have decided to write a book on Suzy Cunningham's murder. It's a good story and one that should be told," he said.

The two sat at the table for a good hour or more. Bruce loved to gossip, and Paul loved to listen. They made a good pair. By twelve o'clock they went their separate ways. Bruce climbed over the fence and down the grass pathway. Paul took the ten-minute drive to the Mangonui shops. He would stop off at the local police station while he was there.

CHAPTER 65

The cat was out of the bag. Lucy watched as her father left his breakfast untouched and ran out the door. Soon it would be all over the school. She was Suzy's best friend. They would think she was a pro too. It was awful. She was still wracked with guilt.

"Mum," she said "I can't go to school now, all the kids will be talking about Suzy. I just can't go."

Mary looked across the table at her daughter. "I will call my sister in Melbourne," she said. "It has been quite a while since we took a holiday and the change will do us all good. I am sure the school will understand. After all you were Suzy's best friend."

"Oh thanks, Mum," Lucy breathed a sigh of relief. "You are the best Mum in the whole wide world."

"Go pack your bags girls. I will let your dad know and book the flights. Barbara will be so pleased to see us all."

The girls left the table with sheer excitement. Not having to go to school was good but going to Australia on holiday was bliss.

Mary had been concerned about Lucy. Ever since Suzy had

gone missing she could tell Lucy was suffering terribly. She could hear her crying at night and she had turned uncharacteristically quiet and withdrawn. She knew her husband would feel the same way as her. Better to take Lucy away from all the stress of the funeral and trial. Her sister had a bed and breakfast with lots of spare room and had been asking her and the girls to visit for ages. She missed her sister too.

She made a few necessary phone calls and booked their flights online. She asked her girlfriend to drive them to the airport. The flights left at three o'clock in the afternoon. They would arrive in Melbourne at five o'clock. It was a four-hour flight, but Australia was two hours behind New Zealand. They would be there in time for dinner. And, better still, they would be away from the media frenzy that was taking over their small quiet town.

CHAPTER 66

Constable Bromley had only one thing on his mind - to keep his daughter's involvement in the case from reaching the press. He had already told Lucy to cancel all her social media websites including Facebook. She could reinstate them after the case had run its course and was no longer of interest to the public or the media.

Mary had called him to say she was taking the girls to Barbara's B & B in Melbourne. He was pleased they wouldn't have to deal with the craziness that was taking over the area.

As soon as he had the case all tidied up he would feel a lot more comfortable. There was a meeting scheduled for ten o'clock with all the teams to review the week's reports. Forensics was in the process of analyzing the girl's panties. He was hoping to find Jenkins' DNA on them so he could finally close the case.

Diane Jenkins had been calling him all morning. She was driving him crazy. Finally he had to tell her, the girl's panties were found among her brother's possessions. His fingerprints were the only ones on the gun, they had photos that Jenkins had taken of the girl and forensics had determined the cause of death was suicide. But she had still been insistent he would not have committed suicide.

"The panties must have been planted on him" she had persisted. "He has been set up. He is all the family I've got. I will contest the cause of death. It should be homicide."

Bromley did feel sympathy for the lady. It was obvious her brother liked young prostitutes. He himself had seen his car near where Suzy was last seen. He was there when they found him dead in his car with the gun by his side. He needed no more proof that Jenkins was not the man Diane thought he was.

Just when he thought he would grab a bite of lunch he saw a man entering the reception area of the station. He walked out to meet him.

"Can I help you?" he enquired.

The man introduced himself as Paul Jamieson. Bromley didn't recognize him as a local.

"I am staying in the cabin at Audrey's place at Hihi," said the man. "I am a little concerned as I understand the man responsible for the young girl's murder was also staying in the cabin." He went on, "If you have a moment I would like to ask you a couple of questions in relation to the landlady, Audrey."

"By all means," said the constable "but I have only met Audrey once. She is new to the area you know."

"Did you do a background check on her when you suspected Jenkins?" the man asked looking troubled.

"No, should I have done? She wasn't suspected of anything in relation to the crime. Do you know any different?" asked Bromley suddenly interested in what the man had to say.

"I don't want to talk badly of the lady," Paul explained "but I did a check on her as I am writing a book on the case and as she is associated with Jenkins I carried out a bit of research on her."

"You are writing a book on the case?" Bromley asked.

"Yes, it seems an interesting case and as it happened when I arrived in town, it is rather opportune don't you think?"

"What did you find about Audrey?" the constable asked.

"She came here from Whangaroa and owned The Three Suites there. A year ago a couple of men were murdered there. Both men had stayed in one of her suites."

"Holy Shit!" said Bromley.

"The police arrested a guy for both crimes. He is now in the Kaikohe Prison – no doubt he will be serving a life sentence." Paul continued.

"So, Audrey had nothing to do with the murders?" Bromley confirmed.

"Doesn't look like it. But it seems too much of a coincidence, doesn't it?" Paul asked.

"Sure does," said Bromley. "But we have no reason to suspect her with relation to this crime. I would say you are pretty safe over there. I wouldn't have any sleepless nights over it."

"Just thought I would let you know," said Paul. "I would like to talk to you about the case when you have officially put it to bed. For my book, you understand..."

"I'll see what I can do" he replied noncommittally.

After the man left, he did a little research on Audrey himself. He looked at The Three Suites website. He made a call to Constable Driver at the Kaeo station who handled the case. Driver told him Audrey was never a suspect. She had been a person of interest during the early stage of the investigation, as both men had stayed at The Three Suites. However, there was no doubt they had the right guy.

Bromley didn't need any interference with closing the case. He would wait and see if Jenkins' DNA was on the panties. If so, he would be left without a doubt.

CHAPTER 67

Bruce Bromley couldn't get it out of his head. Paul had told him about Audrey's past and now he could think of nothing else. He had already suspected Audrey of having something to do with the guy, Jenkins. It seemed odd to have seen them together with a bottle of wine and then a few hours later Jenkins drives up the peninsula and shoots himself. Something just didn't add up.

He had spent the last few nights keeping an eye on things. He was hoping to get something on Audrey and now she had taken off somewhere. Who knows where?

Paul had told him he was going to talk to the Constable at the police station later today. "He's my nephew and a nice guy," he had told Paul. "Jimmy is a good cop."

Bruce planned to talk his nephew tonight and ask him what he thought. He knew they had Jenkins pretty tied to the murder.

Maybe he was overreacting. Audrey had become quite a focus of his everyday life since she moved in next door. In fact, he could even say he was becoming a little obsessed by her. Last night he had watched her climb out of the bath and answer the phone. Her towel was opened as she reached for the phone. He could see her through a crack in the curtains. What a body with those huge boobs. He couldn't get the image out of his mind. He could get lost in those boobs.

CHAPTER 68

"Bitch" Audrey cursed under her breath. She had watched that obese woman's interview on the tele this morning and was glad she hadn't talked to her last night. Obviously, she didn't know her brother very well. He was a rapist and a killer! Audrey would have to make sure she didn't have the opportunity to go blabbing again.

She had tracked her address to a house in St Heliers Bay in Auckland. It had been a long drive – over four hours and now she was looking for a drive-through to grab something to eat. She reached over to the passenger seat and pulled a wig out of her bag. By the time she had entered the drive through she was wearing large sunglasses and a black pageboy styled wig.

"Double Cheeseburger, small fries and hot tea with milk," she called into the mike.

"Please pay at the first window."

She had a sudden thought "Make that two of the same," she said.

It was almost two o'clock and Audrey figured arriving with

hot fries might take the tension off the conversation she was about to have.

Parking her car a few blocks from the house and carrying a large bag she was impressed when she reached the old villa weatherboard style house. It had a wide veranda and literary hundreds of potted plants. Bromeliads of all shapes and sizes lined the path, the steps and created a billboard of color on the deck.

Audrey removed her disguise and looked through the glass panel in the front door as she knocked. She could see piles and piles of papers and magazines in the hallway. Diane must be a hoarder, she thought. Or at least she has some serious emotional problems.

She had seen Diane's car parked on the street outside the house and knew she must be home. She knocked again – louder this time. Finally, she heard a shuffling and suddenly Diane's rather large head appeared from around the door.

"Yes? Oh, it is you," she said recognizing Audrey immediately. "What brings you to my doorstep?"

"You called last night and I didn't get the chance to talk to you, as I fell fast asleep immediately after my bath. I had a meeting in Auckland today so thought I would pop by and offer my condolences and see what it was you wanted to ask me. I haven't had lunch yet, so I brought us some fries and a burger."

Audrey knew she was rambling, but it helped to hide her anger for the interfering woman in front of her.

The mention of fries was enough for Diane to open the door and direct her into the kitchen - the only place that had seating room. The inside of the house looked like an explosion had just taken place. Diane grabbed a couple of plates from a pile of dishes on the bench. Audrey opened up the fast-food boxes and proceeded to place the contents onto the plates.

"I must have some tomato sauce around here somewhere," Diane said looking frantically through boxes.

"Please, don't find it for me. I am happy without it," Audrey said pleasantly. She could tell Diane took the visit as a friendly one. Maybe she needed some quality girl time and Audrey was happy to oblige.

The tea was a little cold and Audrey offered to heat both cups in the microwave. Diane nodded with her mouth full of meat and cheese and pointed to the far corner of the room where there was a microwave disguised as an ironing pile of clothes.

Audrey turned her back and removed her little packet of special mix and added the contents into one of the teas.

"Do you like sugar in your tea?" she asked Diane.

"No just milk" Diane answered with a mouth full of fries. "I am on a diet."

Audrey returned to the table with the hot teas and handed one to Diane. "Nothing like a nice cup of tea to soothe the mind," she said and then added with feigned sincerity, "I am so sorry about Gavin. I really liked him. He seemed such a quiet, respectful man."

Diane began to sob. "He was my only family. He stayed with me for months after his divorce. I should never have suggested he find his own place. He would be alive now."

"He seemed happy in the cabin. He was looking forward to getting in some fishing. I can't imagine what happened," Audrey sympathized.

"It is all a set up. Someone framed him," she cried as she finished her tea. "I will not rest until I know who it was."

Audrey consoled her and comforted her until she saw Diane droop in her chair. Audrey let out a deep long breathe. "Finally," she said. She looked at the time. It was three o'clock. She needed to hurry. She still had work to do here and it was imperative she return to the cottage this evening.

She looked around. "There must be a few unopened boxes of something I can bring back from my shopping trip." She chuckled as she picked up a brand-new toaster, shower organizer and a set of new bath towels.

onstable Bromley had been trying to call Diane Jenkins all morning to advise her they needed the funeral director's name in order to release her brother's body. This was his third message this morning. He tried on her mobile phone and her home phone to no avail. She had already viewed his body at the mortuary and had indicated she would contest the forensics' report stating the cause of death was suicide. She insisted it was a homicide and she would prove it.

Diane had been calling him constantly yesterday and yet today, he had not heard a peek out of her. If he didn't hear from her by tonight he would send a squad car over to talk to her personally. Maybe she was just not answering the phone to avoid the media.

Finally, he heard back from forensics regarding the girl's panties. They were still checking for semen, but they did manage to remove some prints from the fabric, confirming they were a definite match to Gavin Jenkins' prints.

"Yes!" shouted Bromley as he hung up the phone. "It's over." He called in the team working in the station to tell them the news. The case could now be closed and put away in the archives.

His family was on their way to Auckland airport. He was sad to see them go but relieved they would not have to attend Suzy's funeral today. It would be too much for Lucy and the media would be there asking questions.

The funeral was at eleven. Bromley was attending and so was Detective Burt. Bromley attended most funerals in the area. He felt it his duty to show respect for the residents in his jurisdiction. Today was going to be tougher than most. Suzy was only sixteen and she had her whole life ahead of her. The gossip surrounding her prostitution activity had turned her death into a circus. Bromley cursed the government's decision to legalize prostitution in New Zealand. It just gave young girls like Suzy the wrong message. Maybe her death would put a spotlight on teens and prostitution. He hoped so.

CHAPTER 70

Paul had been working on his book most of the night. Obtaining background on all the persons involved in the case was time consuming but necessary. He had confirmed Constable Bromley did have a teenage daughter named Lucy. Finally, he found a photo of her from an old newspaper article and it matched the photo he found on Suzy's Facebook page. He wondered what the media would do with this information. He decided to hold onto to it until he had all the facts. After all he had no reason to suspect that Lucy was with Suzy the night she disappeared.

Today was Suzy's funeral and he was planning on attending. Not only in respect for the young girl and her family but to see who attended. He wondered if Constable Bromley and his daughter, Lucy would be there.

He had also done more research on his landlady. He was sure she had more to do with Jenkins timely suicide than she let on. He just couldn't figure out what. He wondered if she had snooped around in his cabin when he wasn't in. His printer light had been on when he had returned yesterday and he was sure it had been turned off when he left. He decided to add a password to his computer so it was secure in the future.

It was almost midnight when he heard her car crunching up the gravel driveway last night. He could tell she was driving slowly as to not create too much noise. He presumed it was for his benefit. But surely, she could see his lights were on and he was obviously still awake. He had looked through his curtains as she got out of her car, reached in the back seat and removed a few small boxes.

He wondered if she would be attending the funeral this morning. He was sure she would. After all it was her tenant that killed the poor girl.

He decided to call Diane before leaving for the funeral. They had been in touch via email since she returned to Auckland. She said she had called a lawyer and was going to contest the official cause of death. He wondered if she had had any luck. She had not emailed him since yesterday morning. He listened to the phone ring and then her voice mail picked up.

"This is Diane Jenkins. I am not able to take your call. Please leave a message after the beep."

"Diane, its Paul Jamieson here. Just wanted to know how you are and if you managed to contact a lawyer about changing the cause of death from suicide to homicide. Call me back or email me."

It was odd that communication had suddenly stopped between them. He knew she was a solitary person. She had told him so. He thought she would need a friend now. Maybe it was just too much for her. He would try again after the funeral.

He grabbed his keys and made his way to the car. He saw her carrying in firewood on a wheelbarrow.

"Morning Audrey," he called out to her.

Audrey beamed a huge smile. "Good morning to you Paul. You are all dressed up. Going somewhere special?" she asked.

"Off to Suzy's funeral," he said surprised that she had to ask.

"Oh is it today?" she said nonchalantly. "I don't like funerals – or weddings. They both are way too depressing," she added and continued to push the wheelbarrow towards the cottage.

CHAPTER 71

It was just as Constable Bromley thought it would be. The funeral was a circus. It seemed as though every resident within hundred miles was in attendance. School children were gathered outside the local church placing flowers on the lawn. Bromley had never seen such a turn out for a funeral. He was required at time to redirect the traffic coming into the small town. Media trucks were parked along the small rural street.

The service was heartfelt. The school choir sang. One of Suzy's friends played her favorite song on the piano. The Cunningham's were surrounded by family and loved ones. It was such a sad occasion.

At times Bromley looked around the crowd. He saw the guy, Jamieson, who was staying in Audrey's cabin outside looking at the array of white and yellow flowers. Bromley knew red flowers were not appropriate for a funeral as they represent happiness. No more than two colors should be present either.

The casket was closed and covered with a beautiful arrangement of white lilies and white roses. Suzy looked out to the large congregation through a photograph. Her beautiful, long, red hair reminded Bromley of her street name, Red. He wondered how many of her clients were attending her funeral. He couldn't tell from looking through the crowd. Johns came from all walks of life; married men who wanted the kind of sex their good wives didn't provide, single men who wanted quick and easy sex, men who wanted to regain their lost youth and sexual prowess, socially inept men who found it impossible to get a date, commitment free sex – you name it... young girls like Suzy provided it.

He had heard the argument many times that it was safer having sex with a pro than on a date with a stranger. But he also knew older men hated wearing condoms and they actually thought if a pro let them have sex without a condom then they were a special client. New Zealand brothels insist that their girls have protected sex but Bromley knew if guys refuse to wear a condom and they have a pocket full of cash - well the rules tend to be broken.

He wondered how the Cunningham's were coping since they found out Suzy was working the streets. He was sure they were in disbelief. They refused to talk to the media. Not a mention of Suzy's other persona was heard at the funeral. The media kept a respectable distance from the event – he made sure of that.

He heard his name and turned around. It was Jamieson, Audrey's tenant.

"Can I have a word with you?" Paul asked.

"It's not really the time or place," Bromley stated

"It's just Diane Jenkins. I cannot seem to contact her and I am worried. She and I have been communicating since her brother went missing. She is not returning my phone or email messages."

"How long since you last heard from her? he asked.

"Yesterday morning," said Paul.

"I need to talk to her myself," said Bromley. "I will send a squad car to her address. St Heliers bay, isn't it?

"Yes, thanks," said Paul. "Can you let me know if you get in touch with her? I would really appreciate it."

"Will do," said Bromley.

When Bromley returned to the station, he made another call to Diane Jenkins. He left yet another message to contact him as soon as possible. He would wait until tomorrow to send a squad car. He was quite sure Ms. Jenkins was just avoiding answering her phone and picking up messages. After all she was in mourning.

CHAPTER 72

While Paul was out, Audrey decided to mow the lawns. It was another sunny day and the grass had dried out from the storms last week. She liked physical work. It helped lift her mood. As she followed the self-propelled machine along the neatly mowed rows, her mind went to yesterday and her visit to St Heliers Bay.

Audrey liked completing a project. Tying up the loose ends was her specialty. She had stayed on for almost an hour after Diane had succumbed to the doctored tea. It was imperative that it appeared Diane had a heart attack. Only to be expected under the extreme stress she was going through and her obvious over-weight condition. Audrey had become quite proficient with the plant, oleander. Oleander combined with GHB was a lethal combination especially when you are dealing with someone with an existing heart condition.

She had brought with her that day her oleander plant and small trowel and had planted it near Diane's kitchen window. She made sure she covered the area around the plant with existing leaves and foliage from the surrounding area.

Oleander has been used for years to treat heart failure in China and Russia. The plant has also been used to treat diseases from cancer to skin diseases to snake bites and warts. However, an overdose can cause sudden death.

Audrey took her time making the pot of oleander tea. She let it brew in the boiling water and then poured a cup and tipped the contents down the sink. She placed the cup on the table next to an article about oleander tea benefits she had printed out from Paul's computer.

Diane was still seated at the table. Audrey rested her head onto her arms. She looked very peaceful.

After she had ensured that there was no trace of her visit, Audrey left the house, donned her disguise for the last time and walked the four blocks to her car. She never saw a neighbor open her curtains and watch as the dark-haired lady walk by carrying a load of packages.

Audrey dipped into her purse for her phone and cursed as she remembered. She had left it tucked away in the ladies toilet at the movie theatres in Whangarei and would pick it up on the way back to Hihi.

Nothing like a shopping and movie day in Whangarei to blow away the cobwebs – if anyone asked that is. She had already downloaded the movies that were playing there. This was one occasion she actually was pleased that New Zealand was behind the US when it came to movie releases.

CHAPTER 73

The six o'clock news shocked the small seaside Auckland suburb of St Heliers when they heard Diane Jenkins had been found dead earlier that day in her home.

"Diane Jenkins is the sister of the Gavin Jenkins, the man suspected of murdering Suzy Cunningham of Mangonui and who was found dead in his car two days ago. The cause of Diane's death is still being investigated. Police say her death may have been caused by a heart attack. Both Gavin and Diane Jenkins have no living relatives."

There were photos of both Diane and Gavin Jenkins along with a photo of Suzy Cunningham. There was also a clip showing Suzy's funeral the day before.

A pre-recorded interview with Detective Burt and Constable Bromley detailed the events and confirmed that the case of Suzy Cunningham was now closed and no further suspects are being pursued at this time.

Constable Bromley was watching the news and knew they could not give all the details to the media. Forensics had indicated Ms. Jenkins death could possibly have been a suicide and her time of death had been estimated to be between midday and three o'clock that afternoon. They would have final results from the autopsy tomorrow morning.

He had an Auckland team going door to door in the area asking neighbors if they had seen anyone entering or leaving Ms. Jenkins' house. It was a long shot. But one he felt he must pursue.

It had been a long and tiring day. The discovery of Diane Jenkins' body had played hard on Bromley's mind. He even felt slightly responsible for her death. He had been annoyed by her constant nagging about her brother's cause of death and had even avoided returning her calls. When she didn't respond to his recent phone messages he even felt a little relieved. He had hoped she had contacted the funeral home directly and given the instructions regarding her brother's body so he didn't have to be bothered with it. Now he knew she was in no state to be organizing her brother's funeral. He had heard her place was a hoarder's nightmare. Coping with what her brother had done must have put her over the edge.

Bromley spent the night working at the station. He had no one to go home to. He took the time to go over every little detail of Ms. Jenkins' death. St. Heliers Bay Police had emailed him their complete file to date. They were also waiting for the autopsy results.

CHAPTER 74

Paul Jamieson's mind was working overtime. He was distressed to hear about Diane's death.

Constable Bromley had called him this morning. He wanted to know if he had heard anything from Diane the morning of her death. Had she called him? Was there any indication she was planning to take her own life?

Paul had checked his emails and phone messages and there was nothing at all from Diane.

"She killed herself?" Paul had asked in dismay.

"I have just received the autopsy results and it would appear to be suicide. Poison," he replied.

"Oh my God! How awful!" Paul said, shocked at the news.

"Yes, looks as though the death of her brother was too much for her to cope with."

"I know Audrey wanted to keep updated, can you pass on the news to her" asked Bromley.

"You know, Audrey was out all day and didn't return until the wee hours that day" Paul confided. "I know because I was writing until late and saw her car return. Just after midnight if I remember correctly. I thought she might have gone to visit Diane.

"Why would she do that?" asked Bromley.

"Guess I was wrong." said Paul.

The conversation with Constable Bromley unsettled Paul and he decided to take a walk down to the table rock at the bottom of the private road. It was a beautiful spot. An old wooden table sat jammed between the rocks high up over the water. Someone had sprayed the gorse recently around the table and the dry prickly branches were blowing into the lapping tide.

The sun was warm for a winter's day. He watched the fishing boats chugging out to the open sea. A few lone fishermen sat in their small dinghies enjoying the calm waters. The pohutikawa trees were gripping onto the banks - their roots exposed and their branches heavy with leaves. At Christmas time their red bottle-brush flowers would blossom creating a spectacle along the waterfront.

Paul breathed in the crisp cold air and let out a long sigh. He had been excited to write his book. But the death of Diane really made the story personal. He had liked the lady and couldn't accept someone so full of life could now be gone forever. She had been the one to doubt her brother's death was a suicide and now it had been confirmed. Or, had it? Did Bromley suspect that it might be a homicide and why? Were her death and her brother's death too coincidental?

It was time to talk to Audrey. He needed to play his cards just right. She should not suspect he has any doubts as to the two deaths. Maybe he should accept the welcome drink now. He made his way up the beach road back to his cabin deep in thought.

CHAPTER 75

Audrey hunted everywhere. "Where the hell can it be?" she repeated for the hundredth time. Her favorite necklace – a green hand painted piece of pottery attached to a string. She wore it almost every day - even when she mowed the lawns. She knew she was wearing it the morning she left for Auckland. Now it was nowhere to be found. She hoped it had fallen off in the car but a complete search proved this unlikely. She just hoped she had not lost it at Diane's house. Of course, finding anything in the clutter would be almost impossible and knowing it was hers would be downright impossible. She gave up when she heard a knock at the front glass door.

"Audrey thought I might take you up on that welcome drink if the offer still stands," said the amazingly cute Paul, standing there, just staring at her.

Audrey felt speechless. She thought any chance with Paul was less than impossible. Now, there he was, looking so sexy and smelling so good that she could only say, "Why Paul, of course the invitation still stands. Give me an hour and then I will meet you on the garden chairs on the front lawn. Would you prefer beer, champagne or white wine?"

She hoped Paul didn't drink red wine. It gave her a headache and she never had any on hand.

"White wine is great," he said, "See you in an hour."

Paul left and Audrey went into fast mode. Bath, hair, make-up, sexy gorgeous outfit that was casual and didn't make her look too overly dressed for drinks on the lawn.

Audrey popped some chili chicken wings in the oven and a garlic roll. She ripped open a packet of salt and vinegar chips and decided wearing heels on the lawn in the winter wasn't really a good decision. Her heels dug into the soft earth as she headed over to the white-painted, cob furniture and horrors of horrors she tripped and fell face down on the lawn.

A quick look in the direction of the cabin confirmed her worse fears. There he was coming towards her grinning from ear to ear.

"Here, let me help you," said the gallant man.

Audrey was humiliated. "Thank you. I shouldn't have worn heals," she said much too honestly.

"You went down like a lady," he said graciously.

Audrey dusted herself off and together they picked up the bottle of wine, still in one piece, and two wine glasses. Paul poured the wine while Audrey excused herself and went back to the cottage for a complete makeover in thirty two seconds, leaving a shower of potato chips in her wake.

Upon her return Paul stood politely. *Such a gentleman,* thought Audrey.

"Cheers," he said raising his glass.

"Cheers," said Audrey already beginning to giggle with antic-ipation and sheer delight.

"Here's to the memory of poor Diane," said Paul.

"To Diane," she said as she clinked his glass.

Paul studied Audrey's facial expression when he mentioned Diane, but there was no reaction. She looked completely nonplussed as if they were toasting a distant living acquaintance.

He felt a little guilty when he looked at her. She had obviously mistaken his re-acceptance of her drinks invitation as some sort of attraction to her.

"Constable Bromley called me this morning with the news that Diane had taken her own life. He said it was poison," he confided.

"Poison?" she asked "What sort of poison?"

"He didn't say," said Paul wondering why Diane didn't looked at all perturbed that Diane's death was suicide.

"I presume Diane didn't want to live with the shame of what her brother had done," replied Audrey. "Isn't it a beautiful evening," she added changing the subject.

"Yes, you have a lovely view here," he agreed.

"What is your book about?" Audrey asked interestedly.

Paul looked a little taken back at the question. "Still working on the research. It's early days yet," he said wondering if she already knew the answer.

As the sun set over the bay Audrey suggested they go inside the cabin where she had some nice hot chicken wings and a salad. Paul accepted graciously as he followed her across the lawn carrying the empty bottle. His sole purpose this evening was to find out where Audrey went the day of Diane's demise.

Chapter 76

Constable Bromley had been on the phone with Detective Sergeant Morrison in charge of Diane Jenkins' case. He had confirmed it was a mixture of GHB and the plant, oleander that had caused her death. The lethal combination had caused her heart to fail. They had found an oleander plant growing in the garden outside her front window. They had also found traces of the plant in her teacup.

"Have you found anything that might indicate the death was not a suicide?" Bromley asked.

"No. Looks like she was alone during the time of her death. We have been doing neighborhood interviews and the only person seen around the time of her death was a middle aged, dark headed lady walking near Ms. Jenkins' house, carrying a load of boxes. Apart from that nobody has seen anything or anyone it appears.

"What about the oleander plant? Was the tea made from that plant?" Bromley asked.

"Yes, it would appear so. The plant is extremely toxic when digested and Ms. Jenkins, being a diabetic and having a heart condition, the result was fatal. Only three other deaths have ever been reported due to ingestion of oleander as far as we can tell.

It was impossible to do a complete search of the house due to the excessive hoarding. The team had to climb over piles of magazines, newspapers, unopened boxes from hundreds of stores and online shopping companies. A bloody mess it was." Morrison complained. "The women obviously had issues."

"Did you find any more GHB in the house or where she could have got it?" Bromley asked.

"Can't find a bloody thing in that house. Could be anywhere mate. Sorry but I can't help you with that. You can still get GHB easily in Auckland, if you know where to look."

"Thanks, let me know if anything else comes up. I presume you are treating the death as a suicide then?"

"Yes, it seems a pretty open and closed case," said Morrison.

Bromley hung up the phone and sat deep in thought. Something was troubling him.

CHAPTER 77

Bruce and Mary were enjoying an evening glass of wine on their deck. It was getting cold and they decided to go inside and watch the news.

"That poor Diane Jenkins," said Marge. "They say she was a hoarder. Imagine living in those conditions and, on top of that, she finds out her brother murdered that poor girl. I wonder how Lucy is coping, now she has lost her best friend."

"Mary said Lucy was so upset she called her sister in Melbourne and asked her if they could stay for a few weeks until things settle down. I hear Lucy is taking it hard. What with all the talk about Suzy being a prostitute and all." Bruce confided.

"I can't believe that it all happened in our back yard. Didn't you meet that guy, Gavin?" Marge asked.

"No, just Audrey. But I have met the new guy staying there, Paul Jamieson. He is a writer. Writing a book about Suzy's murder. We saw him at the funeral remember?"

The news came on and their attention was directed to the large flat screen television in the middle of the room.

"The death of Diane Jenkins of St Heliers Bay has been

reported to be suicide. The plant, oleander, was ingested along with the drug, GHB, which would indicate a deliberate act of inducing death. Oleander is poisonous to both animals and humans. Its flowers, leaves, sticks and twigs are all poisonous. Even honey made by bees that use the nectar from the flowering oleander is poisonous. The poisonous ingredients are; Digitoxigenin, Nerl, Oleandrin, and Oleondroside. Symptoms include blurred vision and vision disturbances including halos. Death usually only incurs with extremely excessive doses. Symptoms affect the gastrointestinal, heart and blood, nervous system and skin. Usually symptoms only last for one to three days and may require hospitalization. Death is unlikely. The faster you get medical help after ingesting Oleander the better.

"The drug GHB is better known as the date drug. It is a depressant drug that slows down messages between the brain and the central nervous system. At low doses it acts as a sedative. At higher doses it acts like an anesthetic. Its effects can last up to three hours. GHB is almost impossible to detect after death. But hair analysis can confirm the presence of GHB in the body.

"The combination of GHB and oleander proved lethal for Diane Jenkins."

A photo of the common New Zealand oleander plant was on the screen. "I have seen that plant growing in Audrey's garden outside the cabin," said Bruce. "I had no idea it was so poisonous."

"You had better tell her," said Marge. "I would hate her to accidentally ingest it."

"Good idea," said Bruce thinking it was another excuse to pop next door. "I will go over tomorrow."

CHAPTER 78

Audrey wasn't stupid. She knew Paul was writing a book about Suzy's murder. She had read what he had written on his computer when he was at Suzy's funeral. She also learned something very interesting. Suzy's best friend was Constable Bromley's daughter, Lucy. She wondered why the media had not got hold of this information. If Suzy was prostituting herself it was likely Lucy was doing it too. *Bromley must be keeping this information to himself,* she thought. *I wonder why.*

The evening had not gone to plan. All Paul wanted to talk about was the murder - questioning her about what she thought, what she knew, where she was when it all happened, until she had to say, "I have an early morning tomorrow and really have to get some sleep," just to get rid of him. Ok, so he was writing a book – big deal! He obviously thought himself far superior to little ol' Audrey who was so bloody stupid she didn't know his book was about the murder. When, in fact, he was so bloody stupid he didn't know murder was something she liked to do just to prevent boredom. And, what's more, Paul had begun to bore her.

She had got all dressed up for him, provided two bottles of wine, dinner and her company, when he had just provided an evening of constant interrogation. Well, thought Audrey, he can go to hell for all I care and that is exactly where he will be going if he doesn't pick another topic for his precious book.

Audrey headed for the kitchen in her PJs and bed socks. Tip Top vanilla ice cream is the best in the world, she thought as she poured over passionfruit sauce and added a banana for good measure. Given a choice, dessert wins over men every time.

Looking out the curtain at the cabin next door she could see a shadow pacing up and down. Bet he's pissed off, she thought as she sucked on her spoon.

CHAPTER 79

Constable Bromley was putting all the Suzy Cunningham files in a box. He was pleased he could finally put the case to bed. Mostly because now could keep Lucy out of things. Gavin Jenkins did him a favor. Taking the case to trial would have brought out Lucy's association with Suzy and she would have had to testify under oath. The town would know she was with Suzy that night and, for sure, he would be ostracized by both; the public and the police. Worse, Suzy would have to deal with it for life.

The second box was harder to close. He picked up the cardboard lid bearing the name Gavin Jenkins and paused for just a moment before adding the words Case Closed.

Today should be a happy one. He had just talked to Mary to tell her they could come home in a few days. The town had moved on with their lives. It had been ten days since Suzy Cunningham went missing and almost a week since her body was found. Even the media was now focusing on Diane Jenkins' death by oleander poisoning.

He was getting calls from residents worried about the plant

and if their dogs, cats and small children were at risk. Was there going to be a law forbidding the growing of oleander, like there was marijuana?

Oleander plants were common in Northland. He supposed there might even be a couple in his garden he should get rid of before the girls return. They would only remind him of the case and he didn't like the idea of keeping poisonous plants around.

When the phone rang on his office desk he didn't hesitate, "Constable Bromley, Mangonui Police Station" he answered with a revived attitude to life.

"Constable Bromley it is Audrey here." He heard.

"Audrey, what can I do for you?" he asked surprised.

"Well it is a little difficult to talk about on the phone. Can I come down to the station and talk to you?" she asked timidly.

"Is there a problem? He asked now concerned.

"There might be," she answered. "I just need to talk to you."

"Yes, come on down" he said

"Great see you in about half an hour" she said and hung up.

CHAPTER 80

Paul's book was coming together nicely. He had developed his character profiles through his research. He had also been going through Suzy's friends' social media sites and was amazed at how much teens revealed about themselves and their friends. He now had no doubt Lucy must have known about Suzy's prostitution. In fact, there was gossip about Suzy and Lucy having gone to the movies on the night of the murder. There had been a group of girls at the movie that night and they had seen Suzy with Lucy and another, older girl. He would track down that girl somehow. He knew he couldn't talk to Constable Bromley about his daughter. Suzy's friends had tweeted about Lucy having gone to Australia after Suzy's body was found. He had added the information into Lucy's profile along with his suspicions of her involvement in the underage sex business.

Today he would tighten up the timeline of the murder and the two suicides. He hoped to finish the book in a couple of months and get it to a publisher before someone else beat him to it. He liked to print out his draft as he went. He preferred to read off paper rather than his computer screen. He had piles of paper sprawled out all over the cabin. Each pile was neatly categorized.

Early this morning he had taken a walk down to the waterfront to get some exercise and breathe in some fresh air. The walk had done him good. His focus had returned and he knew he could get a full day of writing done.

His thoughts went back to his evening with Audrey. She hadn't given away anything. She just kept that constant, bloody smile on her face and refused to give in to any of his tactics. She had even had the nerve to ask him to leave by saying she needed to get some sleep.

CHAPTER 81

A udrey had seen Paul leave for his walk. She knew she had to be quick if she was going to make her plan work. A quick sort through his pile of papers gave her the ammunition she needed.

She walked into the police station with a feeling of anticipation. This would bring the final curtain down on any suspicions the police may have about her.

Constable Bromley directed Audrey into a small room with just a desk and a couple of chairs. She wondered if it was an interrogation room. She supposed it was.

"Now what can I do for you?" Bromley asked.

"It is about Paul Jamieson," said Audrey. "I invited him over for a drink and dinner last night as a friendly welcome and his conversation has got me worried."

Constable Bromley paused and let Audrey continue.

"He seems to think your daughter, Lucy, is involved in Suzy's murder. He said he has been researching Suzy's friends through their social media sites. He has proof Lucy was with Suzy the night she was murdered."

"What sort of proof are you referring to?" asked Bromley, obviously uncomfortable with where the conversation was going.

"Here," said Audrey as she reached into her handbag and pulled out a wad of papers. "I was so concerned that I went into the cabin this morning when Paul was out walking and copied some of his research and some of the pages from his book."

Audrey laid out on the table various copies of social media chatter, Paul's writing about Lucy and a copy of an article on oleander poisoning.

Constable Bromley looked at the pages, one by one. "Is there more?" he asked.

"Oh yes, he has piles and piles of information on everyone associated with the deaths. He even has your background information and family details," she said. He seems to have a lot on Diane Jenkins. She pointed to the page on oleander poisoning. "He had printed this page out before she even took her own life. How scary is that? Look, you can see the date on the printout."

"Leave this with me," said Bromley. "I will look into this." He added, "What you have done isn't legal. You entered his home and took it without his permission."

"I know," said Audrey looking a little sheepish "I just wanted some evidence to back up my suspicions" she said.

Audrey stood to leave saying, "I feel so much better now. I have been worried. You seem like such a nice man and I don't like what Paul Jamieson is doing. It was bad enough that the poor girl Suzy was killed, but to drag your daughter into it seems wrong somehow. He is like a dog with a bone and won't let go."

"Oh, one last thing," said Bromley "Where were you last Monday between midday and three o'clock."

Audrey was taken off guard. She didn't expect to be questioned. "Mm, she said thinking "Oh on Monday I went to

Whangarei to do some shopping and I saw a couple of movies. I love movies and prefer them on the big screen."

"Do you know where Jamieson was that day?" he asked.

"I have no idea," she said. "I didn't get home until very late and he was home when I got home. His car was there and the lights in the cabin were on," she said.

"So he could have gone out on Monday?" he probed.

"Oh, absolutely. He could have been out all day," she said, grateful his questioning really related to Paul rather than her.

"I see. Well thanks for coming in," he said.

When Audrey left the station she felt like celebrating with a nice glass of Sav and fish'n'chips from the restaurant overlooking the harbor. "It's such a wonderful day," she sighed as she pulled into an empty car park, immediately in front of the restaurant.

CHAPTER 82

Constable Bromley couldn't stop reading the papers in front of him. He must have read each page five or six times. "Fuck! What a bastard!" he kept repeating as the words dug deep into his worse fears. He knew he was trapped. Once the book was released his family couldn't live in the same town. He decided he only had two choices. Ask for a transfer to somewhere in the South Island as far away as possible or find a way to stop Jamieson from printing the book. He, of course, preferred the latter.

He hadn't put the case files in storage yet. They were sitting on his desk. He opened the file on Suzy Cunningham and started reading. He looked at the interviews with Suzy's school friends.

Of course, Lucy was mentioned along with many other schoolmates. However, she had not been interviewed and he wondered why. He guessed it was because she and had stayed home after Suzy's body was found. I guess the case was solved before they had the opportunity to interview her, he surmised.

There was no mention of Lucy having been at the movies that night. The case had focused on finding who picked her up from the shopping center. His interview with Staci was in the file. She had admitted to dropping Suzy off at the shopping center that night. No mention of Lucy being there was on the record - he had made sure of that. If this book got out he would be in serious trouble for omitting this information. "Fuck," he said again. "I have to stop the book."

He looked at the page on oleander poisoning. Why would Jamieson be researching this information prior to Diane's suicide? Did he have something to do with it? Did he give her the information? Could he prove it?

His family was returning in a couple of days from Melbourne. He must fix this before then. He picked up the phone and called Detective Sergeant Morrison at the St. Heliers Bay station.

"Can you email a copy of the Oleander Poisoning information you found at the scene of Diane Jenkins' suicide?" he asked.

"What the hell for?" Morrison asked. "You know we have closed the case here."

"Just tidying up loose ends here," said Bromley.

"Shall do." Morrison obliged. "I'll get the office to email you a copy. Everything OK there?" he asked. "Messy business the Suzy Cunningham and Jenkins' deaths," he added.

"Yes, thanks mate," Bromley said as he hung up the phone and sat staring at the wall. *If they are the same then I have something to work with*, he thought.

CHAPTER 83

Bruce was looking forward to a chance to chat with Audrey. He had already checked for her car from the boundary fence line twice this morning. "Surely she is home now," he said to Marge.

"What's the panic all about?" said Marge. "I think you fancy her."

"Don't be silly," he replied looking a little sheepish. "I just don't want her to poison herself on the bloody plant." As he said it, he felt stupid. Oleanders were everywhere. He just wanted an excuse to see her again.

"You may as well bring her some of my fresh home-made bread," said Marge wrapping a loaf in brown paper.

"Thanks, you're a darling," he said, kissed her on the cheek and headed off across the freshly mowed lawn.

As soon as he reached the boundary fence, he could see Audrey's car in the parking area. There was no sign of Paul's car. He was pleased he would have Audrey all to himself. He climbed over the fence and headed across the new sheep paddock towards the cottage.

She came to the door looking absolutely beautiful. Her hair was swept up in a twirl on her head. Her lips were painted a soft red and her green eyes matched her green necklace around her neck.

"Why, Bruce Bromley," she said, as she opened the door. "How nice. Do come in. I was just about to have a cup of tea would you like one?"

"That would be great," he said, handing her the loaf of bread. "My wife is a great bread maker," he said handing her the brown paper parcel.

"Fresh bread. Thanks. I love it! How nice of your wife," she said, as she sat down at the round, mahogany table and gestured for him to join her.

"To what do I owe this visit?" she asked.

"I don't know if you have been watching the news lately," he said, "but they have been warning people about the oleander plant. It caused the Jenkins lady's death in Auckland and I wanted to warn you in case you have a plant around. I think I saw one when I was visiting with your tenant, Paul, the other day."

"I didn't know you were friends with Paul," she said showing just a flicker of concern.

"Well, I wouldn't call us friends, per say, but we did have a nice long chat the other day. He was telling me about the book he is writing. Quite a project taking on the Suzy Cunningham murder," he divulged.

"Yes, he seems to be completely absorbed with the case. You say you saw an oleander plant by the cabin?" she said. "Can you show me where it is?"

She poured the boiling water into the teapot, and they headed over to the cabin.

"That's funny. I am sure the plant was between that red flax bush and the agave," he said confused, pointing to the gap in the garden in front of the cabin."

"It looks as though the plant has been removed," she said. "Maybe Paul heard about them on the news and decided to dig it out," she said hopefully.

"You would think he would ask you first," said Bruce. "Oh well it is gone now. Good thing too."

Audrey and Bruce returned to the cottage and enjoyed a couple of slices of Marge's bread and the pot of hot English breakfast tea.

"I don't know about Paul," said Audrey. "He has been asking me a lot of strange questions about Suzy's death and, in particular, her friendship with Lucy Bromley. Paul mentioned that you are Constable Bromley's Uncle?"

Bruce nodded.

"He seems to be focusing on Lucy in the book. He also seems to have a close association with Diane Jenkins. All really strange. I wonder if they knew each other, before this all happened," Audrey queried.

Bruce was concentrating on Audrey's huge breasts. He couldn't take his eyes of them. They were the biggest breasts he had ever seen.

Audrey rose from the table and said "I am sorry Bruce, but I have to spray the thistles while the weather is still fine. I hear rain is coming tonight and I want to get the paddock ready for the sheep."

Bruce jumped to his feet. "Of course. I'll let you get on with it," he said as he made his way to the door.

"Thanks so much for stopping by," she said smiling that big smile of hers. "And, please thank your wife for the bread."

Bruce walked back across the paddock to the boundary fence

and made his way home. *At least she invited me in,* he thought. Next time I will go over in the evening and bring a bottle of wine. You never know, I might get lucky.

Bruce whistled all the way home.

CHAPTER 84

Paul was a little annoyed that Constable Bromley hadn't taken his concerns regarding Audrey seriously. In fact, he wondered if Bromley was just relieved to have the case solved. Gavin and Diane's convenient suicides enabled the case to be closed quickly without his daughter being questioned and her involvement being exposed.

He had been writing all day and was feeling like a walk to stretch his legs. He decided to drive down to Cable Bay and take a stroll along the red sandy beach. It was still quite warm and the sun would not be setting for a couple of hours yet.

As he drove down the main highway just before the Mangonui turn off he spotted Constable Bromley's car driving towards him. *I wonder if he is heading to Hihi to talk to Audrey*, he thought as he gave him a wave. The policeman waved back in recognition.

Paul liked living on the edge. He had left school at fifteen and had lived off his wits ever since. He had learned his good looks and disarming charm enabled him to get pretty much anything he wanted in life. It wasn't until recently; time had played a trick on him and women were not as attracted to him as they used to be. He had always been able to get any women he wanted. Having never married he preferred the freedom single life offered. He liked to think of himself as a "toy boy" and excelled as an accessory worn by very affluent older women.

This pampered lifestyle also came with fast cars, designer clothes and platinum credit cards. He had seen the world from the great heights of Machu Picchu to the remote wonders of Easter Island.

In between his relationships he worked online buying and selling shares in the stock market. Since the latest stock market fall he had been struggling financially. His last job working as a business and marketing manager for a New Zealand corporation was obtained through his close association with the owners' wife. He knew as soon as he started with the company he wasn't going to get rich as an employee and had managed to draw a monthly bonus, which was not exactly approved by the management. The owner's wife was easier to charm than her husband and when his little scheme was discovered he took the easy way out.

This murder has been a lifesaver. He would sell the movie rights to the book and have enough money to retire. Things were looking up and Paul, for the first time, knew that finally he was in control of his life. His next women he had sex with would be young and beautiful with a body to die for. This book was his ticket to freedom.

He sat on the sand and watched the setting sun spray orange and red streaks across the darkening sky. The stillness was sublime.

Not even the sound of his phone ringing in the distance would break his trance.

Chapter 85

Bruce Bromley was troubled. He decided to call his nephew and have a chat.

"Jimmy, Bruce here. I don't want to put my nose where it doesn't belong but I am concerned about that guy, Jamieson and the book he is writing about the murder. Audrey says he is all over Lucy being involved with that poor girl, Suzy's death. I don't know if it is because you are the lead cop on the case or if he is just stirring up trouble. But, I don't like it. Tell me Jimmy; was Lucy involved in any way?"

"She did go to the movies with her the night Suzy went missing but came home after the movies. Suzy's friend, Staci dropped Suzy off at the Taipa shops and then she drove Lucy home."

"Is the girl, Staci, likely to talk? Bruce asked.

"We have already interviewed her. She is a sex worker and known by the Kaitaia cops. After Suzy's death she moved to Whangarei. I doubt if Jamieson knows about her involvement."

"I hope not. That would not be good for you or for Lucy. I would suggest you find a way to keep the girl quiet. If Jamieson gets hold of her there is no telling what she will say. Oh, by the way Audrey's oleander plant has mysteriously been uprooted and has vanished. It was outside the cabin. I saw it there a few days ago. Strange don't you think? Audrey thinks maybe Jamieson removed it." Bruce divulged.

"I can't imagine why. Don't worry Bruce. I am on it. I have been doing some digging into Jamieson's past and he is a shady character. Was let go from his last job under some cloud. Seems he lives off wealthy older women. Would be a good thing if he went back to where he came from."

"I agree. I don't like him living next door. I am also concerned about Audrey. She has been through a lot with a murderer living next door and now she has a scoundrel and a womanizer. Anyway mate just wanted to fill you in. When are Mary and the kids returning?"

"In a couple of days. I would like this Jamieson thing sorted out before they return."

"Give them our love when you talk to them next. We miss you guys. Time for a get together," said Bruce.

"Sure is," replied Bromley. "And don't worry about Jamieson, I have it covered."

CHAPTER 86

S taci's phone rang. She didn't recognize the number and presumed it was a new client. "Hello," she answered warily.

"Is that Staci?" she heard.

"Who wants to know?" she answered curtly.

"My name is Paul Jamieson. I am writing a book about the death of Suzy Cunningham and I understand you were the last one to see her that night?"

"What's it to you if I was?" she asked, annoyed.

"I am just trying to get to the truth," he said gently. "Anything you tell me is in complete confidence. If it makes you feel more comfortable, I will tell you what I know and you can simply confirm it."

"It will cost you," said Staci "Nothing is free these days."

"I would be happy to pay you for your time," he said. Why don't I come down to Whangarei and we can meet over coffee?"

"It will cost you five hundred bucks," she said.

"That's a bit steep for a bit of conversation," Paul complained.

"Then it's your choice" she said. "Five hundred dollars or no information."

Paul paused and thought for a moment. "OK then. Why don't we meet at the China Town restaurant downtown at noon? It will take me a couple of hours to drive down there, so wait for me if I am a little late." He looked at the time. It was almost ten o'clock.

"OK see you at noon," Staci hung up her phone and smiled. Five hundred bucks for a conversation. Today is certainly looking up.

Staci had been doing extremely well in Whangarei. Work was good and paid well. In just ten days she had managed to be put on regular staff at the brothel. She enjoyed her work and liked the protection provided by her boss. All johns had to shower before sex. Condoms were a strict rule. The brothel offered half hour and hourly rates.

Staci knew she was in the minority. Most of the other sex workers had chosen the path of prostitution for purely financial reasons. She had read that one third of sex workers had started in their teenage years and child prostitution is aptly named survival sex due to the child's background of poverty, abuse, family breakdown and addiction. Sex with anyone under the age of sixteen is classified as statutory rape. Staci, however, had grown up knowing she wanted to be a sex worker and one day own her own brothel. Yes, the money was good but she enjoyed sex and she liked the power it gave her.

Staci never liked school and left as soon as she could. She had been a sex worker ever since. It was also the only thing she was good at.

She looked in the mirror at the outfit she had chosen to wear to meet the writer. She felt very important being part of a book. She must make sure he would not use her real name. She was proud she could dress straight. In her outfit of tailored pants, designer jacket, wool scarf and Italian boots she could be accepted into any five-star restaurant. Shame he had suggested a Chinese restaurant obviously expecting her to be too slutty for a classier location.

As she was walking out the door, she heard her home phone ringing. She returned inside and took the call.

Inside the restaurant she saw a nice-looking mature gentleman sitting alone at a table at the rear of the room. He looked up at her admiringly but with no recognition. He looked away. "Pompous Fuck," she said under her breath as she walked towards him. "Paul Jamieson" she asked. He leapt to his feet in amazement.

"Staci?" he asked, obviously taken back, "please, join me."

"Now what is it you want to ask me?" Staci asked, enjoying the power she had over the man.

Paul couldn't answer. He had just fallen in love.

CHAPTER 87

Paul had got it all wrong. He sat mesmerized by the beautiful young woman sitting across the table from him. She was everything he ever wanted in a woman. He was more than three times her age, he deduced, but having spent a lifetime seducing older, wealthier women he reveled in the possibility of winning the heart of this childlike treasure.

Staci was talking and gesturing enthusiastically as she described her friend Suzy. She streamed adjectives; kind, thoughtful, friendly, beautiful, energetic...

Paul wondered how a prostitute could be so elegant, eloquent and adorable. He hung on her every word. She told him how sweet Suzy was and how the media had got it all wrong. She did sometimes date older men behind her parents backs but she never was a sex worker.

When Paul asked her about Lucy, Staci said that she only met her the night they went to the movies. Lucy was Suzy's best friend at school. Staci said she had dropped Lucy off home immediately after the movies. Poor Lucy must have been devastated by Suzy's death.

As soon as Paul realized he was going down the wrong track he decided to change the subject and put on his charm.

"Do you enjoy what you do?" he asked.

"You mean prostitution?" she responded boldly.

"Well, yes. Do you work here in Whangarei?"

"At the moment" she said. "But I am opening up my own brothel in Auckland soon and I will be operating the business rather than participating in it – if you know what I mean?"

"When are you moving to Auckland?" he asked.

"Very soon. In a few days," she replied enthusiastically.

"Oh," he said disappointedly. I was hoping you might join me for dinner one night.

"I'm sorry but I obviously work nights. Do you ever make it down to Auckland?" she asked expectantly.

"Funny, you should ask, he said. "I am planning on moving there in a few days myself."

"Now, that is a coincidence," said Staci with a smile.

"Isn't it? he said.

CHAPTER 88

Constable Bromley answered his cell.

"I did what you asked," she said.

"Did he believe you?" he enquired.

"Of course he did," said Staci. "He was like a puppy dog all panting and pathetic. In fact, I told him I am moving to Auckland in a few days. He said he was moving to Auckland also. I guess I must have charmed him," she giggled.

"Good girl," said Bromley. "I have made the transaction for the twenty. Just like we agreed."

"Thanks. I'll keep you updated" she said and hung up.

Bromley breathed a sigh of relief. It was finally over. Staci would keep Paul busy and away from his daughter. He won't know which way is up by the time she has finished with him.

His visit to Audrey earlier in the day was troubling. St Heliers Bay police station had sent through the copy of the oleander plant information he had requested. They also sent a photo of a green necklace found near the plant. He was sure he recognized the necklace as the one Audrey was wearing when he last saw her.

He has an eye for detail and is blessed with a photographic memory of which he has learned to rely upon.

Audrey hadn't heard his car approach over the Happy song playing at full blast. He saw her through the kitchen window and waved.

She welcomed him inside and offered him a cup of tea and home-made banana cake she had just taken out of the oven. It smelled good and the day was chilly. He accepted with pleasure and took a seat at her table.

He noticed that the cottage was an old, tin garage that had been converted into a home many years ago. There had been recent renovations but it was a sorry home for a women of Audrey's financial background. He knew she had built two expensive homes in Whangaroa in the past ten years, both selling for over a million dollars each. Although Tiromoana was a beautiful property the living quarters were certainly rustic to say the least.

"Bruce tells me your oleander plant has gone missing and you suspect Jamieson may have removed it?" he asked.

"I can't believe it," she said. "Why would he remove the plant? I know they are saying that they are poisonous but, for goodness sake, it is not as though we are planning on chomping on it. I liked the plant."

"Have you asked him about it?" he enquired.

"He took off about ten this morning and he is still out," she said. "I will talk to him when he gets back. However, I did find where he had disposed of it," she said. "I found it in the pile of leaves and branches down the bank, on the ridge. It is where I throw all my gardening stuff. I saw it there this morning when I was clearing away the leaves."

"Well, that solves that puzzle," he said. Then added "I was

wondering where you purchased the lovely green necklace you are wearing?" he asked, admiring the one she was wearing.

"Oh, I bought it at a farmers market," she said. "I love it – thank you," she replied.

"I was thinking of getting one for my wife. Do you think they would still have one? Was it the Mangonui or the Taipa Farmers Market?" He asked.

"Oh I think they have them at both" she said. "It is a local artist - each one is individual."

Bromley looked closely at the necklace and realized it was slightly different from the one in the police photo but obviously crafted by the same artist. Meaning that whoever dropped it in Diane Jenkins' garden had purchased it from the Doubtless Bay area. He decided to track down the artist and find out how many she had sold with a similar color and style.

Something was bugging Bromley. The missing plant, the similar necklace, the oleander plant printout.

"You know," she said, interrupting his thoughts "Diane was wearing a similar necklace when I first met her. She must have bought it when she was up here. I remember because we commented that we must have similar tastes."

"Oh, is that right?" Bromley said wondering if Audrey was covering her ass or was simply making conversation.

"Such an awful situation. She seemed like a nice person and was deeply troubled about her brother. What is it I can help you with Constable Bromley?" she asked. "I am sure you didn't stop by for a piece of my banana cake and a cup of tea."

"Bruce told me about the plant and with all the information you provided the other day I wanted to check it out. However, that seems to be a non-issue now."

Audrey smiled, "I'm glad I could help."

Bromley stood to leave, "One last thing. You might want to

do more thorough checks on your tenants. It would appear that middle-aged men tend to go missing or are found dead in your establishments. That can't be good for business."

"You are right," she said. "I will be more careful in the future."

CHAPTER 89

Audrey watched Paul walk into the cabin. He had been gone most of the day. Within ten minutes she saw him carrying his suitcase out to his car. He returned to the cabin and continued removing his belongings.

She watched as he walked towards the cabin.

"Audrey, sorry I have to vacate the cabin. I am moving back to Auckland. My plans have changed. I hope I have left everything as I found it. Here are the keys," he said, passing them to her.

"Oh, I am sorry to see you go," she said.

"You can keep the month's deposit," he said. "And I am sorry for the inconvenience."

"No problem," she said.

As she watched his car heading off down the driveway she wondered what Bromley had done to get him to leave town so quickly. She didn't know and really didn't care. She had made two months' rent in just fifteen days. She had also finished two projects during the same time.

The ringing of her phone interrupted her thoughts.

"Audrey," she announced.

"Constable Bromley here Audrey. Have you by any chance seen Jamieson?

"Oh yes, Constable, he was here but he has just left. He said he had to return to Auckland. He didn't leave a forwarding address. Seemed in a bit of a hurry. Have you tried his cell phone?"

"Yes, it just goes to voice mail. Thanks anyway," he said, careful not to show his relief.

"Sorry I couldn't help you," Audrey said.

"Oh, you have," said Bromley, as he hung up.

Audrey knew it was over. She walked over to her computer and placed the ad:

A Cabin by the Sea
Private, secluded and fully furnished.
*14 acres of native bush * overlooking the*
ocean
Suitable for one adult
$200.00 per week
No pets, No smoking, No children
Owner lives on property in separate cottage

This time she was sure she would find the perfect tenant.

THE END

ALSO BY LEONIE MATEER

THE AUDREY MURDERS – BOOK SERIES

The Murder Suite —Book One

The Cabin by the Sea — Book Two

The Murder Trail — Book Three

Murder in the Family — Book Four

The Murder Trap — Book Five

Murder in Lockdown — Book Six

The Taupo Bay Killings — Book Seven

If you enjoyed this book, I would be so appreciative if you would write a brief review on Amazon. Thank you.

Leonie Mateer

www.leoniemateer.com

About the Author

Puppeteer, children's entertainer, model agency owner, TV talk show panelist, luxury accommodation owner, entrepreneur, product developer, brand developer, storyteller, author, and indie publisher Leonie Mateer has lived a full and diverse life.

Born and raised in New Zealand, Mateer moved to the United States in her thirties to pursue business opportunities. She returned to New Zealand for several years in the 2000s, running a luxury lodge in Northland—which has been an inspiration for her crime series—and now splits her time between Northland, New Zealand, and the United States.

Mateer is known for her huge success as a brand development expert. She received 'Who's Who' awards from both Leading American Executives and American Inventors in the 1990s. As the creator of the brand Caboodles™, a teen girl brand that took the retail industry by storm in the late 1980s and early 1990s, she created a new retail category—the cosmetics organizer category —with Caboodles' global retail sales exceeding US$100 million worldwide.

Ms. Mateer also works in the real estate industry, specializing in residential and lifestyle properties in New Zealand's winterless far north.

Her two daughters and four grandsons live in the United States and are a constant inspiration for many of her stories.

OTHER TITLES BY LEONIE MATEER:

Business:

The Caboodles Blueprint – Turn Your Idea into Millions

Have a Product Idea? – How Many Could You Sell? – a collection of business articles.

Health and wellbeing:

Psoriasis – The Simple Cure – Who Knew?

Psoriasis - Staying Clear - The Healthy Alternative – a must read for any psoriasis sufferer.

Fiction:

"The Audrey Murders" – a seven book series starring Audrey Wetherby, a serial killer living in idyllic small towns in New Zealand.

Children's fiction:

The Magical World of Dantonia

Black Lake

The Bird Boys

Mason's Secret

Tarot Card Online Game

www.readyourownfortune.com

A do-it-yourself game that enables players to read their own fortunes online, anytime, anywhere. Her sixty-three-card deck, based on ancient fortune telling cards, has been deciphered with the assistance of professional psychics.

www.ingramcontent.com/pod-product-compliance
Lightning Source LLC
Chambersburg PA
CBHW072225170626
46813CB00003B/1093